HAMID and the
Palm Sunday Donkey

HAMID
AND THE PALM SUNDAY DONKEY

by *Mary Drewery*

Illustrated by Reginald Gray

HASTINGS HOUSE, *Publishers*, NEW YORK

First American Edition, 1968
Hastings House, Publishers, Inc., New York
Copyright © Mary Smith 1967
First published by Oliver & Boyd, Ltd.,
London and Edinburgh, as A Donkey called Haryat

Library of Congress Catalog Card Number: 67–26848

Printed in the United States of America

Contents

AUTHOR'S NOTE

It takes a long time to produce a book from the time the author delivers the manuscript to the finished product's appearing in the bookshops. When I completed *Hamid and the Palm Sunday Donkey* at the end of October, 1966, its subject matter was as up-to-date as tomorrow's weather. I little thought that within seven months it would have become history. However, six days of fierce fighting in June of this year have brought great changes to the Middle East. As I write, Israeli forces have occupied Old Jerusalem and Jericho and stand on the west bank of the Jordan River. The Hussein Bridge over the river has been destroyed. Whether the old boundaries will ever be restored is at present unknown.

Yet the story is still valid. Wherever there is war, there will be waifs like Hamid. Tourists will still throng the streets of Jerusalem and climb to the top of the Mount of Olives. The same code of law is being administered in the Courts, even though the portrait of Hamid's King may have been replaced by the seven-branched candelabra of Israel. The sun burns as cruelly over the wilderness of Judaea whether Jew or Arab follows the road.

Above all, the Garden remains—a symbol of the love that alone can bring peace to this troubled land.

Purley,
July, 1967.   M.D.

A Map
of Hamid's
Journey

N W E S

THE HOLY CITY of JERU-SALEM

TO MOUNT OF OLIVES
• HAMID'S HUT

TO MOUNT OF OLIVES

Damascus Gate
Herod's Gate
St. Stephen's Gate

CHRISTIAN QUARTER
MOSLEM QUTR.

Via Dolorosa

HOLY SEPULCHRE

Mosque of Omar
DOME OF THE ROCK

GETHSEMANE

The Souq Bazaar
GATE of THE CHAIN
The Wailing Wall

To AMMAN

CITY WALL

Valley of Kedron

GATE OF THE MOORS (DUNG GATE)

¼ mile

ZION GATE

Jericho Road

To BETHLEHEM

A mounted Rifleman of the King.

A Soldier of the Desert Patrol
Circassian Guard
Bashaw Palace

JERICHO
Camel Drover
Bananas

Tomb of Lazarus signpost

Bedouin Camp

AMMAN

JERUSALEM

BETHANY
Inn of the GOOD SAMARITAN
Water

Judaea

River Jordan

Hussein Bridge
The Lowest Spot on Earth

Gypsies

Mount Nebo

Mountains of Moab

Hedjaz Railway

Wilderness

Dead Sea

A Goatherd

A Shop-keeper of the Souq

King's Highway

A Bedouin

Desert Highway

Signpost at

To Jerusalem 22 miles ← T → To Amman 40 miles

junction of Jericho road

A Desert Chieftain

Roads used by Hamid and Haryat ·······>····

Towards Petra—a long way South

To Aqaba

CHAPTER ONE

The Intruder

HIGH on the balcony of the minaret, the muezzin called the faithful to prayer. " '*Allahu 'akbar, 'Allahu 'akbar; 'ashadu 'anna la Ilaha illa' Allah. Hayya alas-sala.* Allah is great. Allah is great. There is no God but Allah, and Muhammad is his prophet. Come to prayer!" The chanting voice rose and fell in a high and penetrating wail that filled the narrow streets and echoed back from the ancient city walls.

Somewhere, a cock crowed. A donkey brayed. Two curs resumed their snarling, snapping quarrel of yesterday. Jerusalem was waking up, the early morning sun setting aflame the great golden dome of the Mosque of Omar.

On the other side of the Kedron valley, however, the garden at the foot of the Mount of Olives was still in shadow, its flowers closed, its gravel walks empty, its ancient olive trees still slumbering. Only the strewn twigs and showered leaves beneath the trees showed where the previous night's violent storm had disturbed its peace. Now the tossing branches were still.

A lizard crept out of the wall and ran with splayed legs over towards the flower-beds. Then it stopped, alert and watchful. Something else was stirring in the garden.

Over the top of the enclosing wall appeared a hand, small and brown and grubby. Then another. A second later, a dark thatch of hair emerged, and two dark eyes as watchful and cautious as the lizard's. When the whole face was above the wall, it revealed itself as belonging to a small Arab boy, who heaved his skinny frame over the wall and dropped lightly

9

on bare feet to the ground below.

The lizard vanished.

The boy straightened up and looked round him curiously.
He had often wondered what lay behind the high enclosing
walls, what led tourists in their thousands to flock through
the gate. It must be something special. Yet there was nothing here but a garden . . . and a church, of course, but there
were churches all over Jerusalem. Churches were not special.

The lizard had appeared again. The boy picked up a stone
and threw it, but he missed and the lizard darted into the
security of a lavender bush.

It was quite a small garden, bounded to the west by the
Jericho road and to the south by the wall of the church. On
the eastern side of its square, a raised and balustraded terrace
gave access to a two-story building. Screened windows hid
any sign of life within. The remaining boundary was the
high wall over which the boy had climbed. For the rest, there
were the neat flower-beds and the olive trees. Eight of them.
The boy counted them twice. He had never seen olive trees
so old. They were of enormous girth, six to eight feet in diam-
eter. Some of them had their branches propped up with
brick piers.

What a fuss to make over trees, thought the boy, for whom
grey-green olive trees were as familiar a part of the Jerusalem
landscape as buttercups would be in an American meadow.

There was a well in the middle of the garden; but when he
had tossed in a couple of pebbles and listened for their dis-
tant plonk at the bottom, there was nothing left that could
possibly interest a small boy. He turned to go.

Then he saw the branch. Quite a big branch, it was. It
must have broken off in the storm. It was heavy, too, as he
discovered when he lifted it up.

Wallah! he thought. A piece of that would be fine for
carving.

But the branch was far too heavy to take away in one piece,

so he brought it down with a crash on the edge of the well. A small piece broke off the end and rolled across the gravel. The crash of the branch shattered the morning stillness. Two doves rose from the cover of the olive trees with a protesting clatter of wings and wheeled high over the basilica, their plumage turning to pure gold as the sun's rays caught them.

The boy had forgotten he was trespassing, but now he dropped the branch and, with a furtive glance round, picked up the small length of wood from the gravel and thrust it into the folds of his *djubah*. Then he scuttled across the flower-beds to the wall. It was not difficult to find toe- and finger-holds in the stone, and he had soon pulled himself up to the coping. He was just about to swing his legs over to the outside when he felt something gripping his ankle.

Startled, he looked down and saw that a powerful hand was holding it—a brown hand, but the brown was of suntan on a fair skin. And below the hand, a muscular forearm emerged from a falling brown sleeve. His eyes travelled down the arm and sleeve to powerful shoulders, a full bushy beard and a pair of startlingly blue eyes that now looked up at him sternly.

"Come down here, you little scamp," said Blue-eyes in Arabic.

The boy slithered back down the wall into the garden. Against the burly figure of his captor, he looked smaller and more skinny than ever. His dark eyes darted anxiously, seeking a way of escape, but there was no evading this big monk, who seemed to have risen up out of the ground and was holding him firmly by the shoulder.

"And why do you come over the wall like a thief when the door is unlocked, you young Philistine? There was I, telling my beads behind the tree yonder, and you come clattering about the garden like Gideon's men and their pitchers. . . ."

The boy wriggled uncomfortably. He had no idea what the monk was talking about. He only knew that the olive wood under his robe was scratchy to his skin.

"I . . . I . . . only wanted to see what was inside the wall, *sayed,*" he faltered.

The bearded face broke into a smile. "And walls are made for climbing over?"

The boy nodded, relieved that this big man seemed to understand the way a boy's mind worked.

"Well, and what do you think of our Garden now you have seen it?" asked the monk.

The boy thought carefully for a moment before replying. "The trees must be very old," he observed. "Are they what the tourists come to see?"

"Yes,"

"Is that all?"

The monk looked down at the puzzled brown face. "I see you don't know the story of the Garden."

"No. Is it exciting?"

"I think so. Would you like to hear it?"

There was really nothing else the boy could do except say yes, and maybe if he showed enough interest, this big, bearded man might forget that he had climbed in over the wall.

"Let us sit on the steps," said the monk. "We had better introduce ourselves, don't you think? I'm Father Gregory."

He spoke with such grave courtesy that the boy felt less uneasy.

"My name's Hamid," he said, with a rush of confidence.

Father Gregory sat down on the terrace steps, hitching up the skirt of his rough brown habit and stretching out his sandalled feet to the sun, which had by now bounded above the Mount of Olives and flooded the Garden with its radiance. Hamid squatted on his heels, Arab fashion, beside him.

"Have you ever heard of Jesus Christ?" asked the monk.

The boy sighed. It was going to be one of *those* stories. No one could live in or near Jerusalem without having heard of Jesus Christ.

"He was a great teacher," replied Hamid, with the indifference of one repeating an often-taught lesson.

"He was indeed," replied the monk. "And He loved this Garden of Gethsemane. He used to come here often with His friends to enjoy the peace and shade after the bustle and heat of Jerusalem."

"Yes," said Hamid, politely bored.

"In fact, He came here to pray the night before He died, and He was arrested here in the Garden."

"I think I've heard this story before," said Hamid, looking longingly in the direction of the gate.

"I expect you have," replied the monk. "But you may not have heard what followed. Jesus prophesied that Jerusalem would be destroyed—and it was."

The boy's head jerked round. "Jerusalem destroyed! But it's hundreds and hundreds of years old!"

"Indeed it is, but, nevertheless, if you had been here nineteen hundred years ago, you wouldn't have seen any of that." Father Gregory waved a brown arm vaguely in the direction of the city walls that crowned the hill on the opposite side of the valley. "It was just a heap of rubble."

"But however did that come about?" asked Hamid, unbelieving. "Was there an earthquake?"

"Not at the time about which I am speaking. There was a very powerful people called the Romans . . ."

"I know!"

". . . who had conquered the whole of the then-known world, including Jordan and all the land that lies between here and the Mediterranean. The Romans had occupied the country for about a hundred years, but now the Jews were in open revolt against them."

"Jews! Here in Jordan so long ago!"

"At that time, yes."

The boy sighed. It was going to be one of *those* stories. No

Hamid spat. Father Gregory ignored it and continued: "The Roman Emperor sent a great army to put down the rebellion. After four years, by the year 70, only Jerusalem was holding out."

"Go on!" Hamid was all attention now.

"General Titus was in command of the Roman Army. He had four legions and cavalry and auxiliary troops."

"Had he any tanks?"

"No." Father Gregory laughed. "Tanks weren't invented until the First World War. But the Romans were very skilled at making war machines of other kinds. They had battering rams, and 'ballistae'—those were giant catapults that hurled huge stones."

The boy's eyes were bright with interest so the monk elaborated further.

"The Roman troops besieged Jerusalem for months. The Jews fought back with desperate courage, hurling blazing oil from the walls on to the attacking soldiers. At last, when the Jews were dying of starvation, the Romans managed to breach the walls on this side and capture the Castle of Antonia. The Jews fought on fanatically—they were fighting for their holy city. But the Romans won the day. They set fire to the Jews' sacred Temple—where the Mosque of Omar stands today. Then they tore down the city walls and reduced every house and building to rubble."

"And this teacher Jesus said that all this was going to happen?"

"Yes. He knew."

"Well!" For a moment Hamid was speechless. "But what has that story got to do with the Garden of Gethsemane?" he asked.

The monk smiled. "Oh, yes, I'm getting away from the point, aren't I? Well, after the siege was over, General Titus had to go off and conquer somewhere else—the Romans were always conquering places—so he left one legion behind to stop the Jews rebuilding the city. That legion, the Tenth, camped on the Mount of Olives."

Hamid's eyes were dark with excitement.

"Right here, on *this* Mount of Olives?" he demanded.

"Yes. It used to be a lovely range of hills in Jesus's day, covered all over with olives and vines and fig trees. But, of course, all these trees were cut down to make scaling-ladders for climbing the walls, to use for camp fires, and so on. The historians tell us that you could scarcely recognize the Mount of Olives afterwards. Every single tree had been felled—except for these eight in the Garden of Gethsemane. Somehow, they escaped. We know that is true, for these trees are over two thousand years old."

"I never knew any trees could be as old as that," said Hamid, wondering.

"We like to think there is something special about them," said the monk. "Otherwise I can't think why the Tenth Legion should have spared just these eight."

"I'd like to have seen the Mount of Olives when the Legion was here," said Hamid dreamily. "All those soldiers. . . . They wore armor, didn't they, and helmets?"

"Yes, and short tunics and cloaks, probably all red and gold. Then they would have their Eagles or standards, with the badge of the Legion. The badge of the Tenth had a galley on it—that's a kind of ship—and a boar."

From within the buildings, a bell tolled. Father Gregory rose.

"That is the call to Matins. I must go."

Hamid rose too, reluctantly now, for he would have liked to hear more about the Romans.

"Do you know any more stories?" he asked.

"Many, many more." Father Gregory's blue eyes twinkled. "There's one about some other people who climbed over a wall—only it was the wall of Rome that time, and a goose saw them, not a middle-aged Franciscan."

Hamid hung his head. He would have liked to confess about the piece of wood under his robe. But Father Gregory was so kind; Hamid did not want to spoil things.

"Thank you for the story," he said.

"You'd better leave by the gate this time," said the monk. "Goodbye, Hamid. God be with you!"

Hamid grinned sheepishly. "Goodbye, *sayed*," he said.

He walked slowly up the steps and along the terrace to the gate. There he paused for a moment, irresolute. Then he pulled out the piece of olive wood and turned back to the garden.

"Father Gregory . . . ," he began.

But the monk had disappeared into the chapel, so Hamid stepped out through the gate.

Traffic was already beginning to roar along the Jericho

road. Now that he was outside the Garden, Hamid became aware of how high the sun had risen since he first climbed over the wall. There was no time to lose. Clutching the wood to him, he scampered down the lane to the main road.

CHAPTER TWO

A Donkey Called Haryat

HAMID turned off the road just before the fruit market, took a short cut straight down the steep grassy slope that dropped to the Kedron brook, splashed through the shallow stream and clambered up the stony slope opposite. He could see his little sister Ferial and her friends already walking sedately along the road to school, balancing their books and satchels on their heads. *Wallah!* He must be late.

He tiptoed round the corner of the rough home-made shack in which his family lived. His mother was shaking the rugs outside and did not see him as he darted noiselessly across to where a drystone wall marked the boundary of a neighboring olive orchard. Hastily he tugged out a loose stone from the base of the wall, revealing a small hollow behind. This was Hamid's secret hiding-place for his treasures. Quickly he tucked the stolen olive wood out of sight, replaced the stone, scurried back through the low doorway of the house and, when his mother came in, was standing munching a piece of the flat Arab bread that she had set out for his breakfast.

"Where have you been all this time?" she scolded. "Your father has been at his work this last hour and your sister has already left for school. You will be late again. Be off with you."

"Late *again!*" echoed his teacher, as Hamid slid breathlessly into his seat ten minutes later. It was not the first occasion he'd been tardy that term.

Hamid sighed. It was going to be one of those days! Everything would go wrong. His attention wandered from the

18

lesson as he hugged to himself the anticipation of carving the new piece of wood.

What could he make this time? There was enough wood to carve something really worth while. But what? He wanted it to be better than the donkeys and camels that the wood-workers in the *souq* turned out by the thousand for tourists. Of course, there were fine pieces to be bought in Jerusalem as well. Hamid had often peered longingly into the windows of the splendid shops in Saladin Street. Here were displayed exquisitely carved figures of shepherds with lambs on their shoulders, and kings in long robes—some with Arab faces, and some with Chinese faces, and some with Negro faces. And little babies in cradles. They were all something to do with the teacher Jesus. Hamid was not interested in the babies, except that the carvings were so lifelike.

His favorite was a king. The figure was only about six inches high but, even on that small scale, Hamid could admire the perfect detail of the elaborate robes, the jewelled crown and the wise old face. The craftsman had used the grain of the wood to indicate the lines and hollows of the cheeks, and every particular hair of his beard seemed to have been carved separately. Come to think of it, Father Gregory looked a bit like that king. But not so old. It was the beard that did it.

Maybe he could carve one of those "eagles" that Father Gregory had told him about—though he had only a vague notion of what "eagles" were. They sounded like some kind of idol the Romans worshipped. He must ask the monk, if he ever saw him again.

Then he was aware of his teacher's voice. "Hamid, I have asked you the same question *three times!* Daydreaming, as usual. You will stay in after school."

The class sniggered, and Ali, who shared his desk, dug his elbow into Hamid's ribs. Hamid scowled. He would have liked to kick Ali under the desk, but it was no good risking

a further detention from the teacher. He would deal with
Ali later. Anyway, he thought consolingly, Ali would not
dare climb over the wall of the Garden of Gethsemane. Ali
hadn't got a friend called Father Gregory. All the same, Ali
did not have to stay in for half an hour after school was over.

Hamid sat, small and resentful, in the hot classroom, writing out the exercise that had been set as a punishment for
him. Flies buzzed on the window-panes and the sun lay in
hot parallelograms on the floor, where it slanted through the
windows. Hamid was not daydreaming now. He was bracing
himself for yet more trouble—from home, this time.

It was his job, as soon as school was over, to help his father.
Work was hard to come by in Jordan, particularly for the
half-million refugees who had flooded into the country when
the new state of Israel was carved out of Palestine. Hamid's
father had been only a boy when that had happened, but
even today he still had no regular work. For the present,
however, he had a job of sorts. It brought in only a few
piastres a day but at least it kept the family from starving.

There was an open site adjoining a new hotel on the
Mount of Olives, only a short distance from where Hamid's
family lived. The hotel proprietor planned to lay out a garden there, and it was Hamid's father's job to pick the stones
out of the ground by hand and tip them on a pile by the
roadside.

Hamid thought that it was a stupid idea. There were so
many stones that if you moved them all there would be no
garden left! The stones were sharp and flinty and cut your
hands, and even when you had removed the top layer, there
were more underneath.

All day long the sun would beat down on the limestone
slopes of the Mount until the dusty roads and the flinty
soil shone blinding white. After school, Hamid would take
the family donkey up the heat-shimmering road to where
his father had piled the stones. There he would load up

the donkey's baskets from the pile and then lead her farther up the hill to where a building site was being levelled. After he had emptied the baskets out on the site, he would ride the donkey back down the hill for a fresh load. It was slow, tedious work, and Hamid would far rather have played after school was out, but the hotel proprietor wanted the ground cleared as soon as possible, so he was expected to help. And today he would be late.

Hamid ran all the way from school to where the donkey was tethered by the roadside. She was nibbling placidly at the thistles that seem to thrive on the arid slopes of the Mount. She blew in gusty recognition as Hamid loosed her rope, and trotted after him.

He couldn't see his father anywhere. Surely he hadn't been kept in so long that his father had already packed up for the day? But, no, the sun had not yet dipped behind the walls of Jerusalem. He ran on up the hill to the building site, but the workmen there said they had not seen his father since midday. Hamid returned to the orchard. He had better get on with his part of the work, anyway. He picked up the baskets that lay beside the heap of stones, but the strap of one of them was broken and you could not load up a donkey with only one basket.

Uncertain what to do, Hamid went home. It was dark in the little shack after the brilliant sunshine outside and Hamid could not at first see anything. But he could hear his mother weeping, and then, as his eyes became adjusted to the gloom, he saw his father lying on the mat that served as his bed.

"What's happened?" asked Hamid, scared.

This provoked a fresh outburst of weeping from his mother. "We shall starve! We shall starve!" she moaned, rocking backwards and forwards in distress.

Hamid looked timidly from one parent to the other.

"It's my foot," explained his father wincing. "The strap

of one of the baskets broke, and a whole load of stones fell on my foot."

"Is it bad?" Hamid avoided looking at the lump under the thin coverlet.

"Bad enough."

"He managed to get home all right on the donkey," said Hamid's mother. "But the foot seems to have stiffened up since."

"It will be better in a few days."

"A few days!" The woman's voice rose in a wail of despair. "You know Mr. Saad won't keep your job open for you. There are at least a dozen men who would be glad of it. We shall all starve."

She began to weep again. Her husband shifted restlessly.

"Silence, woman," he said. "It may not be as bad as we think."

Hamid thought hard. He was unused to thinking very seriously about anything, so his brow furrowed with the effort of concentration.

"I could do your job for you, Father," he said at last.

"You! You're too small," protested his mother. "And, anyway, what about school?"

But there was a hopeful look in her eyes that Hamid was quick to notice.

"I could pretend to be sick for a week," he suggested eagerly, warming to the idea. "I may be small, but I am strong. See my muscles."

He pulled back the sleeve of his gown to reveal a thin arm, which he flexed proudly.

"It might just work, wife," said his father thoughtfully. "Tomorrow is my day off, anyway, and the lad could easily take my place with the tourists. As for the hotel, if he can just keep the job open for me . . . I can put in extra time as soon as I can bear any weight on this foot of mine." He tried to move his leg, but bit his lip at the pain.

"Hooray! No more school!" shouted Hamid joyfully. "I shall be a man. I shall be the breadwinner."

He strutted round so pompously that, despite the pain in his foot, Hamid's father lay back on his bed and laughed aloud.

So it came about that Hamid stood with the donkey the following morning outside the Church of the Ascension on the top of the Mount of Olives.

Below him, the whole of Jerusalem lay bathed in morning sunlight. To anyone less preoccupied with business than Hamid was, the view would have been breathtaking. The close-huddled buildings stretched as far as the eye could see: flat-roofed houses; domes and belfries of a hundred churches; slender minarets and pencil-slim cypress trees; massive, lion-tawny city walls, zig-zagging away to the horizon; and always, blazing in golden splendor, the Dome of the Rock.

But Hamid had no eyes for the view. Along with the vendors of rosaries and necklaces, the postcard sellers and men with color slides, the photographers and swarms of begging children, he was waiting for the tourists, for whom the summit of the Mount of Olives was usually the starting point of their sightseeing.

There were other donkey-men waiting, besides Hamid. They had smart little donkeys with bright red bridles and gay saddle-cloths. Alongside them, Hamid's donkey looked decidedly drab. She had a piece of sacking instead of a saddle, and a frayed length of rope for a bridle. Also, when Hamid slapped her on the rump the white dust of her daily toil between the hotel garden and the building site rose from her coat in clouds. She seemed to sense her shabby appearance, for her head drooped and Hamid had to push and pull to make her move at all.

Here came the tourists, descending the steps from the simple little basilica of the Ascension, that was the oldest

church in Jerusalem. Cameras clicked and whirred. Voices
—many English and American, Hamid noted with satisfac-
tion—were raised in exclamations of delight at the view.

The waiting crowd of Arabs surged round them. "Beautiful rosaries—genuine wood from the Mount of Olives."
"Color slides—all the holy places. Please, you look?" "Baksheesh, baksheesh!"

"Imshi! Imshi! Move along there!" The ever vigilant
policeman on duty on the Mount of Olives hustled the pes-
tering children away from the tourists. Hamid eyed him
nervously but urged his donkey forward, raising his voice
shrilly, "You like your picture on a donkey? Two English
shillings for your picture on a Palm Sunday donkey!"

Hamid knew quite a lot of English, for it is the second
language in Jerusalem. He did not know what "Palm Sunday donkey" meant, but his father had told him that that
was what attracted the tourists.

The other vendors and donkey-men blocked Hamid's
way, and he was in an anguish of despair as he saw one
tourist after another mount his rivals' donkeys and pose for
pictures. An argument arose over change between one particularly thrusting donkey-man and a tourist, and immediately the policeman moved in to sort out the dispute. The
donkey-man argued furiously, but the policeman, stern under his peaked cap, drove him firmly back. Hamid saw his
opportunity to make a bid for custom.

"Two English shillings!" His voice cracked with despera-
tion and disappointment as he saw the guide hurrying the
tourists along, away from the Church of the Ascension and
down towards the Church of Pater Noster. Hamid could see
his customers escaping him.

"Please, lady," he begged, as he caught up with the last
pair of tourists. They had delayed to buy a mother-of-pearl
cross on a fine chain, and the lady was fastening it round her
neck. "Only two English shillings for your picture."

The lady stopped and said something to her husband.

"Really, Harriet!" he protested. "The boy's filthy and so is the beast. Probably flea-ridden, too."

The lady turned and looked at Hamid's dejected figure.

"*Please*, lady." His eyes held hers, pleading. "For you, *one* English shilling."

"All right," she said.

"Sixpence," said her husband firmly.

"Okay, *sayed*. Sixpence." Hamid would have cheerfully agreed even to a penny, he was so relieved to have a customer at last.

He clasped his hands to make a step for her, but he was far too small to give the necessary support.

"Come *on*, Harriet. Do hurry up," said her husband, struggling to heave her on to the donkey's back. "Why on earth you want to be photographed on such an unspeakable creature. . . . There, now you've broken your pendant."

The mother of pearl cross had fallen into the dust. Hamid picked it up and handed it to the lady.

"You come into the picture, too, little boy," she invited him. But Hamid shook his head and ducked behind the donkey.

"Leave him be, Harriet," said the man, unslinging his camera. "Some Moslems don't like their photographs to be taken. I don't know why. Maybe it's something to do with their religion. Ready? Smile! Just a minute, I'll take another."

He gave Hamid a silver sixpence while the lady called Harriet stroked the donkey's nose.

"What's his name?" she asked.

"It is a she-donkey," Hamid corrected her. "But she has no name. A donkey is a donkey."

"In England all animals have names," said the lady. "I know! Yesterday I bought a little wooden donkey just like yours at Fatima's Doll Factory outside Bethlehem. Why don't you call your donkey Fatima?"

Hamid looked shocked. "Oh, no!" he exclaimed. "Fatima was the Prophet's daughter."

"I do apologize." The English lady looked so embarrassed that Hamid felt quite sorry for her. She was such a pretty lady, gay and fair, with gentle eyes, and she *had* been the means of his earning his first money that day.

"I call her Har-y-at, like you," he offered gallantly.

The lady's husband nearly choked with laughter. "You asked for that one, darling," he said.

The lady laughed too. "I really think you ought to have an Arab name for your donkey, but my husband seems to think Harriet appropriate. . . ."

Hamid shook his head after the departing couple. No doubt about it, English people had strange ideas. But he turned over the suggestion in his mind during the morning as he waited in the sun for the tourists. He had plenty of time to think, for he had no more customers that day, even though he dropped his price.

"It's not your fault, Haryat," he said as the pair of them trailed dejectedly down the Mount in the late afternoon. (Somehow, it was easier to talk, now that the donkey had a name.) "You're a working donkey. And, anyway, even if you weren't, we couldn't afford a fine bridle or a saddle for you."

Haryat flicked her ear at a persistent fly and dropped her head to crop a thistle.

"But I suppose I could give you a brush down next week to make you look smarter. After all, you are a white donkey and that's much prettier than being brown."

Haryat made to nibble at a poppy but changed her mind.

"I might even make you a necklace of flowers," pursued Hamid, laying an arm over Haryat's neck. She turned her head and nuzzled his chest. "Not that flowers would last long in this heat."

He walked on, absently. Then, as he passed the building site, he suddenly exclaimed, "I've got it! You shall have your own special necklace. I, Hamid, will make it for you."

He raced over to the building site and rooted round until he found a small off-cut of soft-wood. "Look, Haryat," he said, thrusting the wood under the donkey's nose. "I'll carve your name on here, and you can wear it round your neck on a string . . . like . . . like a *pendant*." He came out triumphantly with the new English word.

CHAPTER THREE

The Find

HAMID found the tile a week later.

His father was still unable to work. Indeed, the foot seemed worse. It was very swollen and hot and throbbed painfully. At least, Hamid thought it must hurt, for his father moaned a lot during the night. It was no good asking him about his foot, for he was quite feverish and seemed not to recognize anyone any more and, although he muttered a lot, none of his words made sense.

Hamid had not been near school since the day of the detention. In his secret heart he admitted he would be only too glad to go back to lessons. Despite his big talk, it was hard work being the breadwinner. He had to force himself to keep at the job, endlessly stooping to pick up the stones and put them in the bucket, endlessly straightening himself and carrying the laden bucket across the garden, down a ditch and up the other side to the pile. No matter how many flints he cleared from the ground, there still seemed to be hundreds left to stub his toes against. Hamid lost count of the number of times he stooped and straightened and walked and tipped the bucket. And filled Haryat's baskets. And walked with her up to the building site. And tipped again. And walked back down the hill to the garden. He would have liked to ride downhill as he used to do when he was still at school—was it only a week ago? But Haryat was a worker just as he was a worker. They were partners. She needed her rest as much as he did.

Rest!

Every night he tumbled on to his mat exhausted. His hands were rough and blistered from handling the stones, and, on the two occasions when he found time to get out his piece of olive wood from its hiding-place and think about beginning to carve it, his hands felt so clumsy that he put it away again.

However, he was not going to admit any of this to his schoolmates. When Ali stopped on the road and jeered at him: "You're not sick. You're playing hookey. I'll tell teacher!"—Hamid pulled himself up proudly and replied, "I've left school. I'm working now." And Ali looked at him with a new respect that made Hamid feel ten feet tall.

He and Haryat became a familiar sight on the Mount of Olives. Day after day they toiled to clear the ground for the garden of the Astor Hotel and still there seemed to be hundreds, thousands, *millions* of stones to move.

The hotel was filling up with guests. Hamid used to see them on the terrace, watching him. Once he heard a man say scathingly, "What a country! Now, if that lad had a wheelbarrow and a plank to cross the ditch, he could do the job in a tenth of the time."

If only he knew! Wheelbarrows cost money. And where would you find a spare plank, when the only trees were a few stunted olives? And where would you find another job if this one were finished too quickly? Hamid would have been glad of a wheelbarrow and a plank, but Mr Saad would not provide them. Not he!

"Haven't you finished yet, boy? Here are my visitors arriving in Jerusalem with every plane, and no garden ready. You tell that good-for-nothing father of yours that I will give him one more week. If he is not back at work then, I employ someone else."

One morning as Hamid pulled at a somewhat larger stone than usual he came upon the tile. In fact, there were several, but all the others were broken. This one alone was whole.

What attracted him first of all was the color. Its terra cotta showed through the crust of grey-white earth. Hamid squatted on his heels and tried to ease the soil off the tile.

There were some marks in a circle. He brushed away more of the soil and spat on the tile to wash it clean. The dampness showed up the pattern more clearly. There were some letters in the circle. Not Arabic letters, which are all flowing curves. These were sharp and angular, like the lettering that marked the Stations of the Cross up the Via Dolorosa. There was a picture as well. Hamid spat on the tile again and traced with his finger the outline of a fat body. A bit like a beetle. No, there was a separate head and the legs were at the bottom, not all round. Whatever could it be?

Something stirred in Hamid's memory. Something to do with Father Gregory. Again, Hamid struggled with the unaccustomed processes of thought. Something Father Gregory had said. About the Romans. And the badges of the legions. That was it! A boar. A boar and a galley for the Tenth Legion.

There was a bit more pattern towards the top of the tile. Excited now, Hamid spat on the tile again and eased off the soil until the outline showed. It could be a galley, he supposed, though it was very faint and crudely drawn.

He set the tile down carefully on the ground and looked across at the forbidding walls of Jerusalem. . . .

Would the city never yield?

The valley echoed with the clash of arms, with shouts and tumult, with the thunder of charging hooves as a messenger galloped up to Hamid and leapt from his foam-flecked steed.

"For you, General Hamid. An urgent despatch from the Emperor."

Hamid dismissed the messenger with a curt gesture. He read the letter, then turned to his aide.

"The Emperor commands us to take the city before nightfall," he said crisply. "Re-group the legions. Bring up the

battering rams! I will lead the attack in person."
A *trumpet brayed from the Mount of Olives. For a moment, the valley hung still . . . waiting. Then . . . "Charge!"
yelled Hamid, setting spurs to his horse.*

If there were guns and armored cars mixed up in that
devastating attack by the Tenth Legion, it was not due to
lack of imagination on Hamid's part but rather to the fact
that soldiers were a part of his everyday life.

There had been an uneasy armistice between his country
and Israel all his life-time and for years before that. Jerusalem itself lay astride the border, and a barrier of wall and
barbed wire divided the city in two. Hamid knew the stutter
of machine-gun fire. There were always troops in the streets
and armored cars patrolling the perimeter of the city. A feeling of tension was always present.

After work that day, Hamid carefully stowed the tile in
his secret hiding-place. To an adult his small treasures would
have seemed a pathetic collection, but he set great store by
them. There was the piece of olive wood, a pen-knife with a
broken blade that he used for carving, two marbles, a smooth,
colored pebble, and a wooden figure of a lizard that Hamid
himself had made. He wrapped them all carefully in an old,
torn *keffiyeh* and tucked them out of sight.

That night, when he lay down on his mat, he could not
sleep, despite his fatigue. His thoughts revolved round the
tile. Round and round. Marching round the walls of Jerusalem at the head of his legions. When was it? The year 70,
Father Gregory had said. But the Christians reckoned years
in a different way. What would 70 be in the Moslem calen-
dar? Oh, it was too difficult. He turned over in bed, but his
thoughts gave him no rest. Could it possibly be a Roman
tile? How could he find out for certain—about the year 70
and whether the tile was Roman? He puzzled and worried
over this problem until, quite suddenly, the answer came to
him. It was so beautifully simple, he could not imagine why

he had not thought of it straight away. Tomorrow morning he would get up early, as he had done that other time. He would seek out Father Gregory and ask him about the tile. The problem settled, Hamid closed his eyes and slept.

Next morning, as soon as the muezzin called, he set out along the Kedron to the Garden of Gethsemane. He was worried as to whether he would be able to find Father Gregory. Did all Franciscans speak Arabic? Or English? There were monks in Jerusalem from all over the world, or so he understood.

However, he was lucky. As he approached the garden gate, he heard the key grind in the lock and the gate was swung open by the very monk he had come to see.

"Sayed . . ." he whispered.

The brown-habited figure swung round and peered at the boy standing outside the gate.

"Why, if it isn't my little Gideon!" he exclaimed.

Hamid entered shyly. Now that he was face to face with Father Gregory, he wondered whether his was a fool's errand.

"I came to show you this, sayed," he blurted out.

He produced the tile from inside his robe and handed it to the monk. Then he stood silently, watching every expression on Father Gregory's face. The Franciscan turned the tile over thoughtfully, brushed his sleeve gently over its dusty surface, and then sat down on the terrace steps and looked at Hamid.

"Where did you get this, boy?" he asked.

"I picked it up in the field next to the hotel. There were many such tiles, but the others were broken. I saw the boar and remembered your story. Is it the badge you spoke of, sayed?" The words came with a rush, but now he faltered and looked up uncertainly. "Should I not have touched it, sayed?"

"No, you were quite right to pick it up." The monk spoke

almost absently, turning the tile over and over in his hands.
"It looks like a genuine Roman tile to me. And that is the
mark of the Legion. See these letters 'Leg. X. F.' The 'X'
means the number ten in Roman lettering. 'Leg. X' stands
for the Tenth Legion and the 'F' stands for 'Fretensis', which
means that the Legion came from 'fretum Siciliense', the
Straits of Sicily."

"Where's that?"

"Oh, a long, long way from here. Have you seen a map of
Europe?"

Hamid nodded. "There is one at school."

"Do you remember a country that looks like a boot?"

"Italy?"

"That's right. Sicily is the island like a football near its
toe. The Straits of Sicily are the narrow waters that run between the football and the toe of the boot."

"I see. What a long way from home the soldiers were,"
observed Hamid.

"The Roman Empire was very big. I think I told you last
time, it stretched right across all the parts of the world that
were known in those days. And right in the center, about

at the knee of that leg we call Italy, was the great city of
Rome, where the Emperor lived."

"An emperor was a sort of king, wasn't he?"

"Sort of, only more important. He ruled over all this great
empire, and anyone who was a citizen of the Roman Empire, even if he had never been anywhere near Rome in his
life, was protected by the laws of Rome. Why, there was one
man who went all the way from Jerusalem to Rome to appeal
to the Emperor against his imprisonment."

"All the way from Jerusalem!"

"Yes. He was a man called Paul—a very famous man who
followed the teacher Jesus. Look." Father Gregory rose and
pointed across to Jerusalem. "You know when you go in by
the Lion Gate into the Via Dolorosa . . ."

"You mean *Bab Sitti Maryam*?"

"I had forgotten. We call it the Lion Gate or St Stephen's
Gate."

"I know it."

"On your left there are some buildings—the old Turkish
barracks—and beyond those, the Dome of the Rock."

"Yes."

"Well, in Roman times, where those barracks stand,
there was a fortress called the Castle of Antonia. Paul got
mixed up in some riots in the temple area and was arrested
and locked up in that fortress."

"Go on."

"He was going to be tried by the Roman governor but Paul
pointed out that he had been born a Roman citizen, way up
in Tarsus in Asia Minor. 'You can't keep me locked up here,'
he said to the officer in charge. 'I'm a Roman citizen. I'm
not going to be tried by any governor. I demand to be tried
by my Emperor. *I appeal to Caesar.*' Those were his very
words. And, do you know, he made such a fuss, they *had* to
take him all the way to Rome to see Caesar. It took months
and months to get there, and he had all sorts of exciting

adventures on the way."

But Hamid's mind was still on the tile. He reached out his hand for it. "If it is Roman, is it valuable?"

"It would be worth something if sold to the right person. Mind you, there must be many such tiles in existence even today. The Legion stayed sixty years here in Jerusalem, and the soldiers would hardly live in tents all that time. They would build barracks and store-houses and stables. They probably had their own brick and tile works to make the building materials, and this symbol would be their trade-mark. So there are, no doubt, many such tiles lying around under the soil of the Mount of Olives, just waiting to be turned up. They are old and of interest, but not as valuable as something like, say, a sword or a shield or a golden cloak-pin. But, of course, if you found anything as valuable as that, you couldn't sell it. You would have to hand it over to the Archaeological Museum."

"Oh, I don't want to sell it," cried Hamid, clutching the tile to him reverently. "It's just that . . . that . . . I've never had anything of value before. I'd like to keep it." He looked up at the sun and rose to his feet. "I must go. I shall be late for work."

"For work? Oh, you mean for school?"

"No, *sayed*," replied Hamid importantly. "I really mean *work*." And he told the monk about his father's accident.

"His foot doesn't heal," he said anxiously. "It pains him all the time, and now he wanders in his head and moans and tosses about all night."

"Has he seen a doctor?"

"No, we haven't any money. And . . . and . . ." The flood-gates opened, and the words came with a rush. "And Mr Saad says if he isn't back at work in a week he will give the job to someone else, and my mother says we shall starve, and I suppose I had better try to sell this tile after all and make some money."

Father Gregory rose. Laying an affectionate hand on the boy's shoulder, he said, "Can you wait five minutes while I collect my medicines? I have some skill in healing, and it sounds to me as if your father has a fever from an infected wound."

"I will wait, *sayed*."

Hamid was alone, a slight, thin, shabby figure in the lovely Garden. All around him was the soft hum of bees among the lavender, and the heady scent of stocks and early roses. He could not recognize the influence of this hallowed place, but he felt its peace envelop him like a blessing, so quiet, so healing, so charged with the love of centuries. He reached out a small brown hand and touched one of the olive trees, so old and so serene. He ran his fingers along its gnarled branch and traced the roughness of its bark with his fingers.

As he touched the tree, he remembered the piece of stolen wood hidden under the orchard wall. Hamid had never before felt this nagging little voice inside him—not about things he had picked up. He did not feel guilty about taking the soft-wood from the building site for Haryat's pendant. Why should this olive wood be so special? Or was it the Garden that was special? Garden or olive branch, they wanted no secrets.

"I'll tell Father Gregory," Hamid decided. "That will make it right."

Then there was the crunch of sandals on the gravelled walk, and a deep, warm voice saying, "I'm ready, Hamid. You lead the way."

He would tell Father Gregory later. Yes, that was best. It was much, *much* more important for the monk to see his father and ease the pain in his foot without delay.

"Let me carry your bag," said Hamid eagerly, his eyes on the precious case of medicines.

Father Gregory shook his head and held out a hand. Hamid put his small, grubby hand into the big, strong one.

"This way, *sayed*," he said.

The early morning breeze riffled the olive trees. Shadows danced on the gravel walks. Apart from the bees among the lavender, the Garden was quiet once more.

Chapter Four

Enter Nicky

Father Gregory came every day to the mud and corrugated-iron hut on the Mount of Olives.

As the monk had anticipated, Hamid's father's injury was infected and had turned septic. When he first called, the whole foot was swollen and inflamed and the patient in a high fever. With skilled and gentle hands, Father Gregory removed the filthy rags that bound the foot, and dressed the wound.

Hamid looked on in amazement as his new friend insisted that all the water be boiled before using it. And the amount he threw away!

"It's easy to tell *he* doesn't have to walk a quarter of a mile with a jerry-can on *his* head!" grumbled Hamid's mother, who regularly fetched the water supply. But she had to admit that her husband looked better, even on the first day the monk attended to him. A spotless bandage on his foot gleamed in the dimness of the hut. The patient was washed and sleeping deeply after some soothing potion the monk had given him.

Each day, when he came to change the dressings, Father Gregory brought a small supply of food for the family, and he showed Hamid's mother how to make an infusion of special herbs to reduce the patient's fever.

The boy followed him reverently, holding the dish of dressings and watching each deft movement of the monk's capable fingers.

"You're very kind, *sayed*," he ventured to say on one oc-

38

casion, but Father Gregory brushed aside the remark.
"I simply carry out what the Lord Jesus has told everyone
to do: heal the sick, feed the hungry."

Hamid looked at him with puzzled interest. This was a
new experience for him. He had learned at school about the
tradition of Arab hospitality, of how the Bedouin would
welcome any traveller into their tents and would feed and
shelter him. But there were no Bedouin in Jerusalem. There
everyone was so busy trying to make a living that no one
seemed to have time or money to spare for the hungry and
homeless.

There was something called U.N.R.W.A., where you
could sometimes get food, but they did not have nearly
enough for everyone. And there were special camps, run by
something else called the Y.M.C.A. But Hamid's father did
not want to be in a camp. That was why he had built the
shack on the Mount of Olives. Maybe this teacher Jesus had
known there were going to be lots of hungry people in Jerusalem in the future, as well as knowing that Jerusalem was
going to be destroyed.

Some new visitors had arrived at the Astor Hotel. Hamid
took particular notice of them because there was a boy of
about his own age. He did not often see European children
in Jerusalem, so he watched the boy covertly as he played
around with a ball on the hotel terrace. He seemed lonely.

Hamid's work that day brought him right up against the
terrace wall. The boy leaned over the balustrade to watch
him.

"Hello!" he said.

Hamid did not know what to say, and he was pretty sure
that, whatever he said, Mr Saad would not like it, so he bent
the more assiduously to his task and pretended he had not
heard. Then the boy's father called, "Come on, Nicholas.
The car's here." And the boy went in.

The following day Hamid returned to school as his father

felt well enough to resume work, so he did not see the English
boy. He was nervous about going back, in case the teacher
was angry with him, but instead he was very kind and seemed
to know all about Hamid's father and Hamid's having to
keep his job open for him. That was something else Hamid
learned that week: that teachers can be reasonable human
beings. He had not had so many new ideas crowding into
his mind for ages.

Perhaps it was the teacher's being kind that made Ali
jealous. Whatever the reason, Ali made a point of needling
Hamid.

"Who said he'd left school? Pet! Teacher's pet!" he
taunted at a break, and everybody laughed. It was harmless
enough, but Hamid knew that Ali was trying to poke fun
at him. He flew at him like a fury, all flailing arms and fists.
Ali was the bigger boy and stopped him with a punch on the
nose that made Hamid's head explode into a myriad stars.
He could feel his nose bleeding, all warm and salty. He
dashed the blood away with his sleeve, but it dropped down
his robe. Ali checked, dismayed at the havoc his blow had
caused, and in that momentary pause Hamid landed two
hard little fists, left, right, into Ali's face.

Battle honors were about even—one gusher against two
black eyes—so Hamid wasn't expecting Ali to return to the
attack. Not that he tangled with Hamid direct; there were
other ways of getting at him. You could pick on his little
sister, for instance.

Ferial was following Hamid from school along the brookside later that day when Ali and his gang crept up behind
her. Flip! It took only the slightest flick to tumble all her
school books from her head into the Kedron. Luckily the
brook had dried up, but Ferial did not notice that. She sat
down on a stone and bawled, with her mouth wide open and
the gap in her front teeth making her mouth look wider open
than ever. The boys all jeered at her.

This was too much for Hamid. Careless of the odds, he launched himself at Ferial's tormentors, which was just what they wanted. Down went Hamid under their massed attack. Feet and fists and elbows and shoulders kicked and punched and dug and shoved. Dust rose in clouds as the heaving mass of boys rolled down towards the dried-up stream-bed. There was an awful rending sound, and Hamid felt his *djubah* tear from his shoulder. A dog appeared from nowhere, and made little darting rushes round the perimeter of the fight, yapping excitedly. Ferial was screaming for help. Hamid wriggled convulsively at the bottom of the pile of bodies. Someone was sitting on his chest and his mouth was full of dust.

"Leave him alone!"

A clear female voice spoke in English, with sharp authority, and almost immediately Hamid felt the boys let go of him. He opened his eyes on the harsh blue of the sky and then shut them against the dazzle. He sat up, shaking his head a little to clear it, and looked round. Ali and his gang had fled, and in their place stood the English boy, Nicholas, and his mother. By their side, her face streaked with tears, stood Ferial.

"It's all right, little girl. They've gone now, the cowards," the lady was reassuring her. It must have been her voice that had stopped the fight. She turned to Hamid. "Are you all right?"

Hamid nodded and scrambled to his feet. He could not speak, for his nose was bleeding again. His *djubah* was ripped right off one shoulder.

"Goodness, you are in a mess! Nicky, give him your handkerchief. There! Now, boy, sit down quietly for a while and the bleeding will soon stop. Just look at your robe!" She rummaged in her handbag and produced a safety pin. "Here you are. Pin yourself up with this. Goodbye. Come along, Nicky."

Kind, crisp and efficient, she stepped briskly back on to

the road and proceeded on her way to the hotel. Nicky, head round to watch Hamid, trailed after her.

"Wasn't she brave!" breathed Ferial, gazing after her in awe.

Hamid wiped the blood from his nose with his sleeve, still too taken aback by his rescue to say anything. Then he realized he was still holding Nicky's handkerchief in his hand.

As if he would stop a nose-bleed with that! It was much too beautiful: a neatly folded square of white linen, with a letter embroidered on it and a piece of tape with red letters stitched to one corner. He would keep it with his treasures . . . or ought he give it back?

Ferial helped him to pin his robe together as best she could, and the two of them went home.

There was no school the following day. Hamid felt he had had enough of stone-picking to last a lifetime, so he faded quietly out of the house at the first opportunity and made for the city. He passed a flock of sheep and goats being driven up to Jerusalem, and turned off the Jericho road on to the approach to St Stephen's Gate. The walls of the city towered fifty feet or more above him. He slipped through a wicket on the left that led into the Moslem cemetery. Huge bushes of prickly pear flaunted their yellow flowers, and lizards, watchful and unwinking, sunned themselves on the tombstones.

Hamid surveyed the massive bastions with fresh-seeing eyes. He could not imagine Jerusalem with its walls pulled down, but, now that he came to look for it, he could see where the walls had been built afresh. Those vast blocks of stone at the bottom—one or two courses of them—must surely be the oldest part. Then there were smaller, but still large, stones, neatly squared off, each one with a border chiselled round it. But the top two-thirds of the wall was made of much smaller, less regular pieces, as if some giant had sorted out all the old broken pieces left over from when the Romans razed the walls and had made the best job he could of building it up again. It made him dizzy, straining to look up to the top of the wall. The golden stone rose sheer, blocking out the sky.

Suddenly he was thrust violently off balance, borne up, swept along. The sunlight dimmed behind a cloud of dust. The air was full of noise and shouting. Hamid cried out with sheer fright, floundered through the bodies that milled round him to the shelter of a tombstone, and hid—from the flock of sheep and goats that was pouring through the wicket gate he had left open!

Wallah! He had better not let the drover catch him!

He crawled behind the tombstone and crouched down. The confusion and shouting went on for some time as the cursing drovers rounded up the flock and marshalled it back on to the road. When at last the hubbub and dust had subsided, Hamid peered over the top of the tomb. All clear!

He approached the wicket gate with some caution, but there was no waiting drover in the lane outside, only a man with a donkey laden with jerry-cans, and a party of tourists, listening while their guide told them about the gate.

Hamid hurried past. Then he had to flatten himself against the wall as an Army jeep shot past him from the military post just inside the gate, zoomed off down the lane and turned up towards Mount Zion. However, once past the post, there was no more danger from vehicles. The narrow street climbed upwards in a series of wide, cobbled steps. On either side the high, blank walls of convents and religious houses turned the narrow street into a canyon.

It was always crowded in the Via Dolorosa. Every few yards there seemed to be earnest crowds of tourists listening to some form of lecture. And on the perimeter of every group, the usual attendance of postcard sellers and curious children, ready to melt into the passing scene if the tourist police approached them.

The crowd parted to allow passage to three burdened donkeys being urged up the steady incline to the *souq*. Their little hooves slipped and clattered on the cobbles, warning a blind beggar descending the street to tap his way to the shelter of the wall.

Here were Greek Orthodox priests with flat-topped black hats and luxuriant beards; Copts with pointed black hats; monks in white habits and sun helmets; monks in brown habits with no hat at all; nuns in black or blue or grey or white, with a bewildering variety of veils and stiff, starched headdresses; and ordinary European men, with their collars turned back to front. For the first time, Hamid began to wonder at the number and variety of Christian sects and costumes and to wonder where Father Gregory fitted into them all.

At intervals alleys led off to the right and to the left, where children played and the thin, wild-looking cats of Jerusalem picked their stealthy way close to the alley walls.

Every few yards a hum of voices and an eddy of tobacco smoke surged from the innumerable cafés where the men congregated to sip mint tea or thick, sweet, Turkish coffee.

Hamid sidled into the pastry-cook's. It was hot as a furnace inside, where Adeeb, his friend the baker, was unloading a batch of flat bread cakes. There were piles of *knaffe*—cornmeal cakes, and *baclawa*—layers of paper-thin crisp pastry stuffed with chopped nuts and sugar and covered with honey. Hamid's nose wrinkled and his mouth became moist as he surveyed the delicious confections.

"*Marhaba!* Hello!" said Hamid hopefully. "Can I do any errands for you?"

"Do you ever?" replied Adeeb with friendly scorn. "Here you are."

He brushed the flies off some battered, stale pastries at the back of the shop and passed one to Hamid.

"Oh, *shookran!*" The boy sank his teeth into the gooey mass. Honey trickled down his chin, and he wiped it away carefully with his fingers and then licked them clean.

He lingered a little while longer, asking endless questions as an excuse to stay, but no more cakes were forthcoming, so he drifted next door. That was the wood-carvers' shop. To Hamid, the *souq* was a compound of exciting smells. Now he savored the tangy smell of sawdust and the pungent odor of glue. He scuffled his bare toes in the rustling heap of wood shavings that curled off in long, crisp ringlets as the men turned on their lathes the little model baskets for the donkey carvings.

One of the men looked up from his work and grinned at Hamid. "*Marhaba!*" he called. They were all used to Hamid in the wood-carvers' shop.

Hamid inched a little farther into the booth. "*Marhaba!*" he replied.

He never ceased to wonder at the speed with which the men turned out the donkeys. A few deft cuts of the power saw, and there would be the little figure. Two sharp taps on the top of a metal die would stamp in the eyes. The baskets were glued on. Another quick dab of glue secured the harness, and there she was, Haryat herself, selling at two hundred or four hundred or six hundred *fils* according to size. All done in a matter of minutes. Whereas the real Haryat had stood patiently in the sun for hours on the Mount of Olives and earned only sixpence.

Wallah! He would do better than that one day! Those stiff little carvings were not really like Haryat, not when you looked at them. Those stamped-out eyes were all exactly alike. Haryat's eyes were gentle, not staring. Her ears were soft and expressive, not standing stiffly up like two spiny aloe leaves. Hamid was suddenly impatient, with the craftsman's scorn of mass production. He turned out of the shop and made his way up through the warren of narrow streets that made up the *souq*.

It was more crowded here and noisier. The smells were more varied too. The booths glowed with color. Plastic sandals from Italy in hectic pinks and blues clashed with hand-painted church candles, richly decorated with roses and stars. Transistor radios from Japan rivalled the local *durkbukkas*. There were gleaming bales of rich fabrics from Damascus, woven with gold and silver thread, jostling for space with sheepskin rugs and gaily patterned carpets, gaudy china and zinc buckets. In one window were imported cameras and watches; next door an artist goldsmith weighed his wares on tiny brass scales while his customer sipped the coffee without which no transaction could possibly be undertaken.

Hamid climbed on up the narrow street. He tried a cheerful *"Marhaba!"* on the lemonade-seller who was stalking impressively towards him. Cups clattered against the huge brass container of lemonade which was strapped to his chest. Tinkling bells proclaimed his wares. The greeting was ignored. Hamid pulled a face at his departing back and nearly knocked down another blind beggar in the process.

"Muta'assef. I'm sorry!" he muttered, backing away. His nose was immediately assailed by new odors, savory and delicious. A stall-holder was making fresh sandwiches, slapping spicy hot minced meat and eggplant between flat cakes of bread. Sales were brisk, and Hamid knew from experience that there was no hope of wheedling anything out of that one. He wandered over to the fruit stall in the hope that one of the colorful pyramids of oranges or melons or tomatoes might be so delicately poised that the mere draft made by his *djubah* in passing would dislodge something. But the fruit merchant had his eye on Hamid.

"Imshi!" he said sharply. Hamid beat it.

He turned a corner and pushed past a pedlar with a tray of sweet green almonds for sale. Pigeons fluttered down and pecked boldly where sacks of dried beans and chick peas had spilled over on the paving stones. Flies buzzed round the hanging carcasses in the butchers' booths. A hubbub of traders' cries, mingled with chatter in a dozen different languages, filled the narrow streets.

Hamid was by a butcher's booth when he first noticed the English boy and his parents. There was a fishmonger's booth near by as well, with some tired and elderly fish adding their odor to the pungent smells of the *souq*.

The Europeans were descending the narrow steps that lead down from the roof of the Church of the Holy Sepulchre. Hamid had ventured up there once himself and peeped at the black-faced Abyssinian monks who live and worship up there. The contrast between that strangely quiet corner of Jerusalem and the bubbling cauldron of excitement that was the *souq* must have been shattering. Little wonder that Nicky's mother was holding a handkerchief delicately to her nose as she picked her way through the jostling crowd.

"Charles, Nicky, do let's get out of here quickly!" Hamid heard her say and saw the tall husband shouldering his way to her side. The crowd closed in behind them, cutting off the boy. He should have kept up with his parents, but like Hamid he was fascinated by the color and life of the *souq*. He stopped and unslung his camera. There were murmurs of protest, but the boy seemed unaware of them. He was focussing on a Moslem woman who was passing. She protested, pulling her thick black veil to cover her own face and that of the baby she carried in her arms. Nicky seemed unaware that her protests were directed towards him. He followed her movements with his camera, and Hamid tensed himself for what he knew would follow.

The crowd turned on the English boy, jostling him and shouting protests. Scared, Nicky tried to back away, but he was hemmed in. He looked round wildly for his parents but could not see them. Hamid wriggled and fought his way

through the throng of bodies just in time to see an arm reach out and grab the English boy's camera. Nicky clutched at it, and the label attached to it came away in his hand. The camera disappeared—but not before Hamid had marked down the arm that grabbed it as belonging to Hassan, the Armenian who kept the ironmonger's shop next to the fruit stall. But there was no time to worry about the camera. Hamid knew the swift, hot temper of the Jerusalem crowd. The English boy could be in real trouble.

Hamid dashed forward and deliberately caught at the edge of the fruit stall. Over went the trestle, and oranges and melons and tomatoes and eggplants went rolling in all directions. The fruit merchant shouted with rage and alarm. People began scrabbling for the fruit, and in the confusion Hamid grabbed the terrified English boy by the arm.

"Come!" he said urgently, dragging him into the crowd.

"Stop those boys!" A cry went up from the stallholder.

Hamid and Nicky plunged on recklessly, blundering and twisting through the press of people.

"Stop those boys!" The cry pursued them down the narrow alley. A man blocked their path. The boys ducked under his outstretched arms and ran on. Nicky skidded on a squashed lettuce and blundered into a stall of poultry. Crates of chickens toppled over, their catches flying open as they fell. Baby chicks were everywhere, hopping and fluttering and squeaking with alarm. Nicky would have stopped to pick some of them up, but Hamid dragged him away and round a corner into the Street of the Chain. They flattened themselves in the first deep doorway they came to and stayed there, panting. They heard the chase come up to the corner and pause. It was a crossroads. Either the pursuers abandoned the chase or went the wrong way, for no angry runners came past their doorway.

Hamid peered out cautiously. The street outside was quiet. He beckoned to Nicky.

"Safe now, I think," he whispered. "Come. We go back hotel."

"But my parents . . ." protested Nicky.

"Not through *souq*."

Hamid set off down the street. Nicky followed, overflowing with thanks and apologies and explanations.

"It's my own fault. They'll be frantic when they can't find me. Daddy told me not to take photographs in the *souq*, but I forgot. Now I've lost my camera. He'll be *furious*."

Hamid nodded sympathetically. "You safe now," he said. "Come. Long way to hotel."

He led on through a series of narrow alleys. He passed the Jews' Wailing Wall with no more than a contemptuous glance and made for the Dung Gate and the road that leads round Mount Zion.

Gone were the busy, colorful scenes of Old Jerusalem. Here were clusters of shell-blasted houses, with a few wretched-looking families moving about where they had established some sort of homes among the ruins. The road dropped down steeply to the Kedron valley.

Nicky had recovered his composure by the time they joined the Jericho road. He was back in familiar surroundings now.

"What's your name?" he asked.

"Hamid."

"Mine's Nicholas."

"I know."

Nicky fumbled for one of the three Arabic words he had so far managed to learn. "Er—*shookran!*" he ventured timidly. "Thanks awfully for helping me."

Hamid flashed him a delighted smile. "*Afwan*—you're welcome," he replied.

CHAPTER FIVE

On Trial

ALL that day Hamid's thoughts kept returning to the English boy and his camera. Hamid squatted, chin on fists and brow furrowed, watching the terrace of the hotel. Neither Nicky nor his parents appeared.

I wonder what his father will do? Hamid thought. He could make no comparisons with his own experience for he had never had anything even remotely as valuable as a camera to lose.

If only he could have stopped the Armenian this morning! If only he had been five foot seven with a pale English face and a clear authoritative English voice, like Nicky's mother, maybe *he* could have said to the Armenian, "Leave that camera alone!", the way she had done when she stopped the boys sitting on Hamid's head by the brookside. But he was not fair or English or five foot seven or grown-up. His height was no more than four feet and a little bit. And instead of being fair, he had a mop of dark hair, eyes black as coal, and a face that was more often than not streaked with dirt.

But he *did* know who had the camera! That Armenian. Hamid knew him all right. He had a squint in one eye that gave him an evil, leering look. It frightened Hamid, that eye did. That was why he had never asked him if he could run any errands for him, in case it was a real evil eye. The man would sit in the doorway of his shop, fingering his nervous beads, running them over and over in his fingers, and looking round with that queer, two-ways-looking glance, and Hamid and his friends would run off as fast as they could.

What if the camera was still in his shop? The more Hamid thought about it, the more certain he became that the camera must be there. Evil eye or no—and here, to ward off its influence, Hamid touched the blue marble he was playing with— he would go to the shop and look.

It never occurred to him that he ought to consult with his father or Nicky's father before setting out on such a hazardous venture. He did not think at all, beyond the need to restore the camera to its owner.

He went back to the *souq* in the late afternoon. He was a little worried in case the fruit merchant should recognize him as the boy who had overturned his stall, so he disguised himself in his only other clothes: a faded yellow T-shirt with *Cub Scouts of America* emblazoned across the front, and a pair of blue jeans. Both garments were several sizes too large for him, but his mother had been given them at a distribution of second-hand clothing for refugee families. Thus attired, he walked hurriedly past the fruit merchant's stall, sidled up to the Armenian's shop and peered in.

There were a lot of things in the window: saucepans and buckets, and saws and shopping bags and brass coffee-pots and big flat platters of woven raffia. The trouble was that they completely obscured the view into the shop. And the doorway was screened by a curtain of plastic streamers. If he wanted to check whether the camera was there, he would have to go inside.

He thrust his hands deep in the pockets of his jeans while he thought that one out. His hand closed over the broken pocket-knife. He could ask how much it would cost to sharpen the blade and whether he could work off the cost by sweeping out the shop or maybe delivering something. That would give him time to look round. He need not look the Armenian in the eye. His hands felt clammy with nervousness, and he wiped them on the seat of his jeans.

At that moment the plastic curtain parted and the Armenian came out. He did not even notice Hamid but threw a word to the fruit merchant, who was serving a customer, and crossed over to the barber's.

There might never be a better opportunity. Hamid looked cautiously up and down the street. There were a couple of tourist police some twenty yards away, but they had their backs towards him. Everyone else was busy. Hamid slid between the plastic streamers and entered the shop.

He was quite alone inside. His heart hammered in his chest. Thump! Thump! He was sure they would hear it outside. He looked round the shop. The walls were lined with shelves to the roof, with more buckets and more coffee-pots and more saucepans. There were boxes as well, with names written on the outside: nails and screws and brackets and hinges. Where was the camera? Might the shopkeeper have hidden it? There was not much light, and Hamid was so nervous he could scarcely concentrate. But he saw it at last, on a shelf at the back of the shop. He was absolutely certain it was Nicky's. It had the same shiny brown leather case, with a bit of string still tied to the strap where the luggage label had been torn off. That little detail had stuck in Hamid's mind.

It was a high shelf and Hamid had to strain on tiptoe to reach up to it. He could . . . just . . . reach . . . the camera . . . with the tips . . . of his fingers. His nails gripped the sides of the case, and he edged it forward. A quarter of an inch. Half an inch. Now he could reach it better. It was coming. There! It was on the edge. He could really grasp hold of it.

Oh, *wallah!* The strap was caught in something! Frantic now with haste, Hamid jerked at the strap to pull it free.

Crash! There was a sound like ten thousand tin cans tied to the tails of ten thousand stray dogs! It was as if all the garbage cans in Jerusalem had been overturned by all the hungry alley-cats!

The strap had caught in a large tin box of nails and had pulled it off the shelf onto the floor. The resounding crash set every coffee-pot and saucepan and bucket vibrating with protest. A clattering shower of nails shot all over the floor of the shop.

Hamid was petrified with fright. For a whole five seconds, he stood in the pool of nails, terrified, unable to move. Then, clutching the camera to him, he made for the door.

The scattered nails were sharp to his bare feet and, before he could make good his escape, the fringed curtain parted and the fruit merchant from next door stood in the entrance. Hamid tried to duck past him, but the man caught him and held him firmly by the wrist, shouting over his shoulder for the Armenian to come.

His shouts attracted the tourist police, and soon Hamid found himself surrounded by big hostile men, all talking at once and accusing him of stealing the camera. He tried to explain, but nobody would listen to him, and, before he knew what had happened, he had been hustled along to the police station. His father was sent for and came limping into the station, and Hamid was charged with the theft. He was terrified and bewildered and desperately unhappy.

Then they went home and Hamid's father was terribly

angry and gave Hamid a beating, and that made Ferial cry too. It was an awful evening, with Hamid crouching silent and miserable in a corner of the hut and his mother and father talking endlessly round and round and over Hamid's crime. What would Mr Saad say if he heard about their disgrace? What would happen to the stone-picking job? What would happen to Hamid? Would he be sent away? Would he be expelled from school? How could he do such a thing? And, as soon as he tried to explain, they both started up again and told him not make things worse by lying.

Torn alike by his mother's distress and his father's anger, poor Hamid tossed wretchedly on his bed that night, unable to sleep and terrified of what the following day might bring.

Daybreak came at last, and a few choking mouthfuls of breakfast, before setting off for the court house where Hamid was to appear.

Hamid was quite bewildered by the proceedings. He had to stand in the middle of the room, and his father was allowed to sit on a chair behind him. There was a table on a dais where the magistrate sat, an elderly man with a grave, intelligent face. There was another man sitting at a table, writing and writing, and there was a little box where the two policemen came and swore on the Koran and told their story. The magistrate asked them some questions. Then the fruit merchant and the Armenian came, one after the other. They swore on the Koran too and told *their* story, pointing to the camera that lay on the table in front of the magistrate.

Everybody talked and talked, and the man at the table wrote and wrote. It was hot, and Hamid did not understand a word of what was going on. There was a fly buzzing round and round the fruit merchant's bald head, and Hamid felt that if it settled he would be all right and if it didn't, he wouldn't. He felt tight inside and screwed up with apprehension. So he forced himself not to look at the fly and instead looked at the big colored photograph of the King that hung on the wall behind the magistrate's chair. The King was very young and handsome in his Air Force uniform, and Hamid thought he looked as if he would understand.

Now the magistrate was talking to him and inviting him to come up on to the dais beside him. Hamid went up very nervously. He had never been so close to such an important person before, and he noticed that the magistrate was wearing a beautiful grey silk tie and that he had a tuft of black hair sticking out of one nostril.

"Do you know about Allah?" he was asking Hamid; and Hamid nodded dumbly, unable to speak.

"And do you know what Allah does to people who tell lies?"

Hamid nodded again.

"Do you ever tell lies?" the magistrate asked.

Hamid hung his head. "Sometimes," he whispered almost inaudibly.

"I want this to be one of the times when you tell the truth, Hamid," said the magistrate firmly, but quite gently. "Now, tell me in your own words exactly what happened.

Hamid looked up. The magistrate's eyes were much kinder than you would think from down there in the center of the room.

"Go on, Hamid. It's your turn to talk now. Don't be afraid. Begin right at the beginning, and tell me why you were in the shop with the camera."

He had not said, ". . . why you *stole* the camera." Someone was prepared to listen. Haltingly at first, but gathering confidence as no one interrupted him, Hamid told the magistrate everything. He told him about the fight with Ali and the nose-bleed and Nicky's handkerchief; how he had seen the trouble beginning in the *souq,* and how that man over there (pointing to the Armenian) had snatched the camera. He told him how he had rescued Nicky and all about how he thought he could get the camera back.

Then the Armenian butted in and said Hamid was a thief; but the magistrate told him to be quiet and not to interrupt.

"And you say that this English boy could prove your story to be true?"

"Yes, *sayed*."

"Do you know where he is staying?"

"At the Astor Hotel, *sayed*. His name is Nicholas."

The magistrate said something over Hamid's head to the writing-man, and the writing-man nodded and spoke to a policeman, and everyone started talking in official-sounding words like "remanded for one week," "further enquiries," and so on.

And Hamid found himself out in the street with his father. The policeman was saying something about having to come back to court the following Monday, so it still was not over and he still might be sent away, and he would have another whole week to spend worrying about it.

Hamid trailed miserably after his father down the street from the court house and on into Saladin Street. Opposite Herod's Gate, his father stopped.

"I must have a coffee," he said to Hamid. "This morning has really upset me. You run on home and tell your mother what has happened. You'd better be excused from school for the rest of the day."

Only too glad to escape, Hamid fled down the broad road that ran round the outside of the city walls, crossed the Jericho road, and slithered down the grassy bank to the Kedron. He was desperately worried and longing to unburden that worry on to someone.

He was about to climb up the other side of the Kedron to his home when he paused. In the distance, he could see the nine cupolas of the Church of Gethsemane gleaming in the morning sunshine against their background of cypresses.

Father Gregory would understand. He might even help.

It meant disobeying his father again and risking another beating, but it was worth a chance. Hamid broke into a run, and the white dust spurted behind his heels as he sped along the brookside to the sanctuary of the Garden.

CHAPTER SIX

Flight

AT FIRST Hamid thought it was not the same in the Garden of Gethsemane. He had not been there so late in the day before.

He paused with dismay as he saw two Franciscans, deep in earnest conversation, pacing the terraced walk that led from the gate, and tourists everywhere, strolling between the olive trees and peering down the well. *His* well, he thought fiercely.

Yet it was the same, for when the monks turned at the far end of the terrace he saw that one of them was Father Gregory. He always seemed to be there when he was needed.

He saw Hamid at once, noting the drooping, dispirited figure and the troubled face.

"What is it?" he asked, leaving his companion and coming across to the gate. "Is your father worse?"

Hamid shook his head and gulped back the tears that were welling up inside him. "It's me," he whispered. "I'm in trouble."

Father Gregory was not shocked or even surprised. "Then you have brought your trouble to the right place," was all he said. "Come. Let us sit in our usual place on the steps and you can tell me about it."

So they sat down in the sun as if no one were there in the Garden except them, and soon there *was* no one there except them, for the party of tourists drifted in ones and twos up the steps and along the terrace to the gate, with no more than a mildly curious glance at the oddly assorted

pair. Once again there was no sound except the hum of the
bees among the stocks and the soft swish from where a gardener was raking the gravel walks at the far side of the
Garden.

Strangely, Father Gregory used almost the same words as
the magistrate had done. "Now, Hamid," he said, "begin
right at the beginning, and tell me what is troubling you."

Once again Hamid spilled out his story, and although it
was rambling and at times hard to follow Father Gregory
did not interrupt. He let the boy work it out for himself in
his own way, and all the time he was watching Hamid's
face and the deep-black eyes that were fixed so pleadingly
on his own.

When at last the boy had finished his account, it was
Father Gregory's turn to speak. "If you have told me the
truth, Hamid, then you have nothing to fear. The English
boy and his father will appear in court to support your story,
and that will be the end of it."

He paused. "You *are* telling the truth, Hamid? You really
didn't mean to steal the camera?"

"No!" The boy's denial was firm enough.

"There's still something you haven't told me, Hamid."
The monk searched the boy's face. "Have you stolen before?"

The dark eyes slid away from his and dropped. The boy's
shoulders drooped. "Yes, *sayed*, many times." It was no
more than a whisper. Then—it had to come out this time:
"Only little things—an orange, an old bit of wood. Things
like that. But . . ." He hesitated. "I once stole something
from here."

There! It was out at last, and now Father Gregory would
drive him from the Garden and there would be no more
talks about the Romans, no more visits to the shack on the
Mount of Olives. Father Gregory would be his friend no
longer. He waited, dumb, for the blow to fall.

"I'm glad you have told me at last, Hamid." The boy

looked up in surprise. Father Gregory's voice was warm and gentle, as always. "Oh yes. I knew you had taken the olive wood. I saw you when you broke the branch and put the piece under your robe. I have been waiting all this time for you to tell me."

"Then you're not angry?"

"Not angry. Only sad."

That was much worse. Hamid burst into tears. "I . . . I . . . wanted some wood to carve, and wood is so hard to find and so expensive to buy. I didn't think an old branch would matter. I'll bring it back. I will. I'll go and get it now."

Hamid rose excitedly to his feet, but Father Gregory pulled him down again. "No, Hamid," he said. "I want you to keep that wood for your very own, and I want you to carve something special from it. But I hope that every time you look at it, you will remember where the wood came from."

"You mean I can keep it? Oh, thank you, *sayed*, thank you." Hamid paused. "But I still don't understand why an old piece of wood like that is so important."

Father Gregory looked away from Hamid and let his eyes wander lovingly over the Garden, over the nodding fragrant flowers and the ancient, silver olive trees.

"Can you feel the peace of this place, Hamid?" he asked.

"Oh yes, *sayed*. There's something special about it." So he had been right. Father Gregory felt it too.

"We of the Christian faith like to think that that peace comes to us as a special blessing because Our Lord walked and suffered here in this Garden. These trees witnessed that suffering and so they are very dear and precious to us."

Hamid only half understood what the monk was saying, but he realized it was something important. He kept very quiet.

"Christians come in their thousands from all over the world to this Garden, but for every person who visits it there must be many thousands who will never have the opportunity. So we try to send a little of the Garden to them. The very leaves of the trees are carefully collected as they fall and used like this."

Father Gregory opened his missal and produced a fold of paper. On the outside was a colored picture of a man on his knees by a rock. An angel hovered over him, holding a cup towards him. Inside was a written message and a single pressed olive leaf.

"Who is that?" asked Hamid, pointing to the kneeling figure in the picture.

"That is the man you call the teacher Jesus; we call Him Lord. He died a very cruel death on a cross to save mankind from sin. That is why we remember Him by a cross."

The monk turned a page of the missal and produced a bookmark. It was very pretty, decorated with pressed wild flowers. In the center, surrounded by a sun-burst halo of gold, was a cross made from fine slivers of wood.

"That cross," said Father Gregory, touching it lightly with his finger, "is made of wood from these trees. Each branch that falls is carefully saved, to be turned into precious souvenirs like this one. They have no money value, but they are greatly treasured by those to whom they are sent."

Hamid looked up into Father Gregory's face. "But you could make *millions* of these out of my piece of wood," he protested.

Father Gregory smiled. "I don't think that wood will be wasted," he said. He rose to his feet and the boy rose with him. "Don't worry any more, Hamid. I'm sure it will turn out all right. Just tell the truth to the magistrate. I will pray for you," he added simply.

Hamid ran back along the brookside with a lighter heart. Father Gregory was right. If Nicky and his father confirmed his story, the magistrate would have to believe him.

His mother was not at home, so Hamid went down to the

roadside in the hopes that he might see Nicky. He knew that he usually came back to the hotel with his parents in the middle of the day. He squatted on his heels in the dust and waited. The sun rose higher and higher until its blinding brightness stood overhead. He ought to have taken Haryat up to the tip, but he felt that maybe his father did not want anything more to do with him that day, so he stayed where he was by the roadside, patient, unmoving, watching.

Big American-style taxis roared up to the hotel and deposited their passengers, but not the blue Buick which Nicky's father drove.

Perhaps they had gone out for the whole day. Hamid prepared to wait the whole afternoon if necessary. The sun passed its zenith. The heat glared blindingly from the white stones.

Hamid's father came down from the field with Haryat. He merely nodded when Hamid told him he was waiting for Nicky, and limped wearily back to the shack. Hamid felt terribly guilty; his father looked so old and tired.

The shadows lengthened, and then, quite suddenly, at about six o'clock, the sun seemed to drop out of the sky behind Jerusalem and was gone, leaving only a silhouette of domes and minarets against the afterglow.

They would not come now. The guests always returned by sundown. Maybe he had dozed and missed them? Hamid did not think he had, but he had to be sure. It was so desperately important that he saw Nicky and his father and told them about the trial.

Summoning up his courage, he approached the hotel. There was no one in sight, so he scampered up the steps to the front door. There was a long glass panel in it, and he could see the lobby, with its spotless mosaic floor, and a room beyond, with a carpet as thick as the ones in the Mosque of Omar. It was all beautifully clean and shining, like the new saucepans in the Armenian's shop. There were

two guests in the lobby talking to Mr Saad, and they were beautifully clean too. Hamid looked down at his shabby robe, clean enough for the hearing in court that morning but now streaked with dirt. He looked down at his grimed feet and for the first time was aware of how he must appear to other people.

At that moment Mr Saad looked up and saw Hamid's small face peering through the glass door. He excused himself to his companions and came across. Hamid did not wait for him. He retreated down the steps to the front gate.

Down in the road once more, he decided to try the back way instead. He had come to know Fuad the cook when he was doing his father's job with the stones. Fuad used to give Hamid scraps from the kitchen.

Steam was eddying through the windows, and the kitchen door was wide open. Hamid stood in the entrance, goggling at the great piled dishes of golden chicken pieces gleaming under the fluorescent light, at the mounds of smoking rice, at the bowls of sliced tomato. But for once the succulent odors roused no desire for food in Hamid. He was too concerned to find Nicky.

"Fuad!" he whispered urgently, as the chef bustled importantly round the tables, checking the orders the waiters were taking up to the dining room.

"Fuad!" Hamid called more loudly; and this time the chef heard him and turned.

"Not now, Hamid. Can't you see I'm busy?"

He turned back to his duties. "How many, Salah?"

"Six—and the lady says she wants only a small portion."

Fuad arranged the chicken on the plates, and Salah bore them away, dexterously balancing four on one arm and hand.

"*Please*, Fuad. It's not anything to eat. May I ask you something?"

"Oh—all right. But don't get in the way." Fuad had no sons of his own, but he loved children and felt sorry for this waif of a refugee boy.

"You know the English family—with the boy Nicky . . ." Hamid began.

"I don't know the guests. I only feed them," laughed Fuad. "They are so many appetites to me. Mrs. Small-Portion-by-the-Window. Mr. Second-Helping-Every-Time, her husband. Miss Can't-Eat-Arab-Food, and so on. I know their stomachs, but I don't know their faces or their names."

Hamid giggled in spite of himself, but he was quickly solemn-faced again. "I felt sure you would know."

"He's probably the one I call Three-Helpings, but I rather think he's left."

"Left!" echoed Hamid dully.

"I'll check. Hey, Salah," Fuad called to the waiter, who had returned from the dining room with a fresh order. "Have you an English boy among the guests?"

"We did have," replied Salah. "But they checked out this morning."

"This morning!" Hamid was aghast.

"Yes, after breakfast. They were going on to Jericho—
staying at Mr. Saad's other hotel there, the Winter Palace."
Hamid's face registered his dismay.

"What's the matter, son?"

"I . . . I . . . wanted to speak to the English boy. It's terribly important."

"Oh, they're coming back."

Relief flooded Hamid's face. "When?" he asked eagerly.
"Tomorrow?"

"Oh no, not as soon as that. Not before Sunday at the
earliest. I can check at the desk if you like."

Hamid shook his head dumbly. He could not speak for
the misery that rose in his chest like a big, hard, knotted
lump.

Not before Sunday at the earliest! And he wanted them
in court on Monday. They might be too late. They might
not even come back to Jerusalem. They would never confirm his story now. He would be sent away. Maybe to prison. Maybe for years. Hamid's terror mounted as his imagination took over. As it did that night in bed.

He could not sleep. He fretted and fretted until his
imagined predicament was out of all proportion to the crime
of which he was accused. Father Gregory was wrong. They
would not believe him, even if he did tell the truth. It was
all the fault of that beastly piece of wood. He could have
it back. Everything had gone wrong since he had brought
the wood home.

But even as he muttered that to himself, Hamid realized
it was not entirely true. He would not have met Father
Gregory or heard about the Romans. And his father might
still be off work if it hadn't been for Father Gregory. In
any case, nothing that came from a Garden as peaceful as
Gethsemane could possibly be evil. As he thought about the
Garden, he grew calmer and began to think more clearly.

He must find Nicky. It was as simple as that. Salah said

he was in Jericho at the Winter Palace hotel. Hamid had never been to Jericho but it was only twenty-two miles away. He knew that. He had read it on the signposts. If he rode Haryat he could surely get there in a day, for he had heard it was downhill all the way. Even if it took him two days for the return journey, he would still be in plenty of time. He had a week before the hearing. He would set off tomorrow. With this decision made, Hamid fell asleep.

He awoke just before dawn and managed to slide out of the hut without disturbing either Ferial or his parents. He knew he ought to tell them where he was going, but he knew equally that if he did they would forbid his journey. So he snatched a furtive piece of bread to eat on the journey, collected his little hoard of treasures from the hole in the orchard wall, untethered Haryat from the stake to which she was tied, and, as the first rays of the rising sun turned Jerusalem into a city of gold, the boy led his donkey up over the top of the Mount of Olives and took the road to Bethany.

CHAPTER SEVEN

The Jericho Road

HAMID paused on the summit of the Mount of Olives. In the distance rose the Mountains of Moab, all pink in the morning sunlight and slashed with purple shadows. At their foot and looking so close that Hamid felt sure he could have shied a pebble into it, lay the Dead Sea, deep, deep blue. Jericho was near the Dead Sea.

Pooh! It was not very far. He could do it in a morning, he and Haryat.

He mounted the donkey and urged her forward. She trotted on willingly, pit-a-pat, pit-a-pat, for the morning air was fresh and cool and the way before her was downhill. She had enjoyed a nibble of dew-laden grass and cornflowers while Hamid was surveying the view.

The road was rough through Bethphage and there was no one about save two road-menders, who were already at work, shaping stones.

"*Sabah al-khayr!* Good morning!" cried Hamid to the workmen as he passed.

"*Sabah al-khayr!*" they replied. "Where are you off to?"

"I'm going to Jericho," boasted Hamid to the men.

"By yourself?"

"Of course."

"It's a hard road for a young boy."

"We shall manage it easily, Haryat and I."

Hamid patted the donkey's neck and checked that the *keffiyeh* full of treasures was still safe where he had pinned it to Haryat's sacking.

"A donkey called Haryat!" laughed the men. "That's something new! Well, good luck to you. You can't miss the road. It's the only one."

"That's good," said Hamid. "I'll be on my way."

"*As-salaam alaykum!* Peace be with you!" called the roadmenders.

"*Wa alaykumu as-salaam!* And unto you, peace," replied Hamid courteously.

He joined the main road from Jerusalem at Bethany. There were a few more people about. A woman was drawing water at the well. The proprietor of the shop where the cars park for tourists to see Lazarus's tomb and the Church of Mary and Martha was setting out his stall with postcards and bottles of Coke. But there were no cars yet to disturb the peace; only the white doves cooing softly in the church garden, where sweet peas, Canterbury bells, loquats, lavender and lilies spilled in a riot of color over the wall.

The road from here to Jericho was broad and new. It had been constructed recently, to replace the old twisting track that looped off to left and right in a series of hairpin bends. But even the new road was very steep.

There were a few stunted trees, and a little grass on which donkeys were grazing. Hamid looked around him with eager interest; he had never been so far away from Jerusalem before. An hour went by. The interest began to change to unease as the road plunged on downwards, one long bend succeeding another, so that the view ahead was always closed by fold on fold of bright, white hills.

The sun bounded up the sky and its fierce heat blazed down on this wilderness of Judaea. Here there was little or no grass. Black goats grazed on sparse scrub that stuck up stiffly through the stony ground. The rocks flung back the heat, as when Adeeb the baker opened his oven door. Only today the oven door never shut. The air grew hotter and hotter and hotter. It was very still.

There were *wadis* running down through the hills, but
the streams were dry at this season. Hamid had never con-
sidered it could be so hot or that he could be so thirsty.
Stupidly, he had not thought to bring water.

A truck ground up the steep hill, its engine laboring.
There was no other sign of life.

Cliffs rose on either side of the road. Hamid felt very
small and vulnerable as he and Haryat rounded a thrusting
shoulder of rock. What if there were robbers waiting to trap
them? There used to be brigands on this road until quite
recently. He had heard about them in Jerusalem. They said
that since the King had built the new road, he had cleared
out all the brigands. But there might be some left!

Then the road began to rise again, and as Hamid reached
the crest of the ridge he could see a huddle of low buildings
to the right of the road. Maybe he could get a drink there.

He turned off the road, slid from Haryat's back, and led
her into a sort of courtyard. It was tumbledown and littered
with heaps of stones, but there was a man there with three
laden donkeys. It was a relief to speak to another human
being.

"*Marhaba!*" said Hamid. "Can I get water here?"

"Surely," replied the man. He indicated a kind of raised,
stone platform in the middle of the courtyard. There was a
hole in the middle of the platform and a bucket with a long
rope attached to its handle.

Hamid lowered it carefully. It was a long way down, but
at last he heard the soft plash as the bucket reached the
water. He hauled up the bucket as fast as he could. It was
heavy, but that did not matter. Here was water, cool and
sweet. Hamid knelt down and drank the water greedily. He
plunged his face into it and splashed it over his throat and
wrists. He felt something butt urgently into his side and
was aware of Haryat, trying to take her share. He drew
back, suddenly ashamed.

"Oh, Haryat!" He turned a stricken face to the donkey. "I have drunk first, and you have done all the work."

He carried the bucket over to a stone trough in the courtyard and poured water out into it. Haryat followed him and began to drink greedily.

"What is this place?" asked Hamid of the man with the donkeys. "It seems to be in ruins."

"It's known as *Khan Hathrur*," replied the man. "But the Christians call it the Inn of the Good Samaritan. It is a good place for water. There are cisterns in the rock underneath here that men say have supplied water since the days of the Romans."

"Doesn't anyone live here any more?"

"There's a police post. That's one of their horses over there."

Hamid had not noticed the beautiful grey that stood patiently in the shade of the wall. He kept very still while a policeman in the distinctive saffron *keffiyeh* of the mounted patrol came out of the post, mounted the horse and rode off. Hamid wanted nothing to do with policemen until he had found Nicky.

"Is it far to Jericho?" he asked at last.

"Far enough, in the heat of the day. Are you alone?"

Hamid nodded. "I have business there," he added importantly.

The man looked at his small shabby figure and at small, shabby Haryat. He was suddenly angry. "What are your parents at, allowing you to travel this road by yourself? And where is your water bottle?"

"I . . . I . . . dropped it." Hamid could not let his parents be blamed.

"Here, take mine." The man unslung his bottle and handed it to Hamid. "No, lad," he said, as Hamid protested. "I only have to go as far as Bethany. I'm nearly home."

He rose then, gruffly dismissing Hamid's thanks, and led his string of donkeys out on the road.

"*As-salaam alaykum!*" he called.

"*Wa alaykumu as-salaam,*" replied Hamid.

He moved on himself shortly afterwards, having first filled the water bottle. He unpinned the *keffiyeh* and transferred his treasures to Nicky's handkerchief. It seemed a pity to soil anything so beautifully smooth and clean, he thought, as he pinned the handkerchief to the sacking, but he needed the old *keffiyeh* to protect his head, like the policeman and the man with the donkeys. He had no *agal* to hold it in place, but he draped it over his head and shoulders as best he could. The man's angry outburst had made him a little afraid.

The road plunged on downwards, blinding white. There was more traffic now, fast cars and taxis with braying horns, tearing down the hill, swerving violently to avoid rocks and boulders that had hurtled down from the cliffs on to the road below.

Haryat plodded on, ears drooping. Hamid drooped on her back. The sun stood directly overhead and Haryat's shadow shrank almost to nothing. The white rocks flung back the sun's heat. Hamid stopped to eat but the stale bread nearly choked him, so he just took a drink from his water-bottle. He poured a little into his cupped palm and tried to give Haryat a drink as well, but his hand was small and the water trickled through his fingers and was wasted on the parched ground.

Presently they came to a notice by the roadside. Its green enamel was chipped and rusting, but Hamid could read the notice that said in Arabic and English, *Sea Level—Mediterranean Datum.* Whatever that meant. The only sea Hamid knew apart from on maps was the Dead Sea, and as he rounded a bend he could see that glittering in the distance below him. It still looked very near, just as it had from the top of the Mount of Olives. It must be some trick of the light.

A line of low, black tents came into view, where some Bedouin had pitched their camp in a fold of the hills. It would be cool in the tents, but the camp was too far off the road. Better to press on.

There were camels grazing on the thorny scrub, and more black goats. One of the camels wandered across the road, bringing the traffic to a screaming halt. Horns blared, the fanfare echoing back from the rocks. Haryat started. She did not like traffic. Or camels. Her nose wrinkled. Hamid did not like camels either, for that matter. They had such disdainful faces, always thrusting out their lower lips in scorn because, unlike man, who knows only ninety-nine names of the Prophet Muhammad, they alone know the hundredth.

The afternoon wore on. Hamid had another drink from the water bottle, and this time he succeeded in giving Haryat a little. Her big tongue tickled his palm, and she nuzzled gently at his robe, as if to say "Thank you." They rested for half an hour and then started on again. The sun arched over the heavens and Haryat's shadow began to move ahead of her.

At last the distance opened out into a vast expanse of flat plain. A ribbon of green wound across it to where the great slash of the Dead Sea reflected the brilliance of the sky. Away to the left lay a pool of emerald, and almost immediately Hamid came upon a signpost pointing to a side road which swung off in the direction of the emerald pool.

With eager hope, Hamid paused at the signpost. His ears were buzzing with the change of altitude and his eyes were blurred with the dazzle of sun on rock, but he could read the legend on the pointing arm. *Jericho*, it said.

The last two miles into the city seemed endless. Haryat was so tired she could hardly put one tiny hoof in front of

another. Her soft ears drooped, her head trailed and every
few yards she paused to nibble at the herbage by the roadside. Hamid sat listlessly on her back. He was nearly asleep.
Their joint shadows marched alongside them, now stretching long and unnaturally tall across the level plain, now
standing up against the palm trees that had begun to line
the road.

They passed the huge Y.M.C.A. camp on the outskirts
of the city, but Hamid was too weary to notice anything
about it other than the fact of its existence. He was anxious
to reach the Winter Palace before dark. Already the sun
was sliding behind the Mount of Temptation, that looms
hugely over Jericho.

Lights sprang into life along the road as he entered the
city. It seemed like something out of a fairy tale after the
day's grim journey through the wilderness. Mimosa trees
lined the roadside, standing among pale gold pools of fallen
blossom. The evening air was heavy with the fragrance of
jacaranda and lemon. Even in the half-light of the afterglow,
Hamid could see the lush groves of bananas and date palms,
oranges, and lemons. This was a fat land, a prosperous land,
far more lush than anything he had ever seen in and around
Jerusalem.

The streets were busy, donkeys jostling for space with
jeeps. A boy crossed the road carrying a stem of ripe bananas
on his head, like one of those stiff headdresses the nuns
wore in Jerusalem. From the cafés and the tables outside
came the hum of men's talk and the mingled fragrance of
coffee and tobacco. High up in Jerusalem, once the sun was
down, it was always cold, but here in Jericho, over eight hundred feet below sea level, the air was still and balmy.

For the first time for hours, Hamid felt like eating. He
gave Haryat a drink at a horse-trough in the street and
squatted beside her, tearing hungrily at the piece of bread

he had brought from home. Although it was stale and not very appetizing, it went down well enough with the help of a swig from the water bottle. Besides, everything tastes better when you know your troubles are nearly over, that the target you have set yourself is almost achieved. They were both weary, Hamid and Haryat, but the very urgency of his mission drove Hamid on. Let him find Nicky first; then he would rest. He forced himself to his feet and, leading Haryat behind him, set out to find the hotel.

It was not difficult. Everyone knew the Winter Palace.

"A few hundred yards along the road on the left. You can't miss it."

The hotel lay back from the road. The garden was luxurious with palm trees and roses. Hamid tied Haryat to a street lamp outside. He did not trust her with roses after the day they had had. If she could eat thistles with relish, what havoc might she not wreak among these trim flower-beds?

Hamid brushed ineffectually at his robe in a half-hearted attempt to smarten himself up. Remembering Mr. Saad, he made his way round to the back of the hotel. He felt sure he could talk his way into the kitchen, particularly if he mentioned Fuad in the kitchen of the Astor.

Ten minutes later he was out on the pavement again. He had a piece of bread and a lump of *lebne*, soft white goat's-milk cheese, in his hand. But he was not eating. He could not eat for the tears that were washing two pale runnels down his dirty face.

Nicky had gone. Yes, he had certainly stayed there the night before. The family had visited the Dead Sea and the caves at Qmran and come back to the hotel for dinner. But they had left that morning, early. No, the kitchen staff were not sure where they had gone. They thought, to Petra and then on to Aqaba.

Hamid moved mechanically to where Haryat was tied and

as automatically set off blindly up the road. He did not know where he was going or what he was going to do, except that he could not go to Petra or Aqaba. They were nearly two hundred miles away across the desert.

CHAPTER EIGHT

Haryat Shows the Way

No DISASTER seems so hopeless after a good night's sleep. And to wake up in a banana grove, as Hamid did the following morning, to find an ample breakfast hanging above your head is luxury indeed. Sunlight dappled the ground where it filtered through the thick canopy of banana leaves.

Hamid sprawled with his back against a tree trunk and munched his way through three bananas. Haryat cropped the grass contentedly. Despite Hamid's having turned off the previous night, in his despair, into the first quiet grove he had come to, she had stayed near him all night.

What should he do now? Hamid laid out all the facts and reviewed them. He was accused, wrongly, of stealing Nicky's camera. Father Gregory had said he would be all right if he told the truth. Father Gregory had further said that Nicky would confirm Hamid's story. Nicky was not available. Therefore Nicky could not confirm his story. That left only the truth. Would that be sufficient?

Hamid shrugged, with a gesture that held all the fatalism of his race. *"Insh'Allah.* If God wills it."

He rose to his feet resignedly. There was nothing for it. He must go back to Jerusalem.

He picked some more bananas. There were so many, the farmer surely would not miss three or four. Then he led Haryat back on to the road. There were even more people about than last night. It would have been pleasant to linger but he should not delay if he were to reach Jerusalem before nightfall.

Hamid shuddered at the prospect of that awful wilderness through which he must climb. Well, at least he had the water bottle. He filled it carefully at the first opportunity, drank deeply himself and made sure that Haryat did also. He decided he would walk for as long as he could and ride Haryat only when he was really tired.

He was walking quite briskly back through Jericho when, out of nowhere, a dreadful thought came to him that stopped him dead in his tracks. If Nicky were not available to confirm his story, might not the magistrate think that Nicky himself was a person made up by Hamid?

He went cold with fear, despite the warmth of the morning. He was at a fork in the road where a signpost he had not seen in the dusk the night before pointed right to Jerusalem, twenty-two miles, and left to Amman, forty miles. He sat down at the foot of the signpost to consider this new aspect of his problem.

If Nicky did not exist, of course, Hamid could not produce him. Turn that back to front and it became: if Hamid could not produce him, then Nicky did not exist. The magistrate would not, *could* not believe him, even if he told the truth. He did not know what happened to boys who stole. He would probably be sent to prison for years and years and years, and he would never see Haryat any more, or his mother, or his father, or Ferial. And Ali at school would be sorry he had given him a bloody nose. Hamid could even see the magistrate as he sentenced him. His eyes were no longer kind and he had grown enormously, so that he loomed over Hamid just as that cruel-looking mountain over there loomed over Jericho.

"I sentence you, wicked Hamid, to be locked up in prison for the rest of your natural life."

Someone else had been locked up in prison. Someone Father Gregory had told him about. He had been locked up in the old Turkish barracks . . . well, where the barracks were

now. Paul. That was the name. Lucky Paul! He had not had
to stay in prison in Jerusalem for the rest of his life. He had
managed to get away to Rome. Paul had appealed to Caesar.
Paul had appealed to Caesar! Hamid stood up and looked
at the signpost again. Amman. The King's palace was in
Amman. Why should not he, Hamid, appeal to his King,
just as Paul had appealed to Caesar? *He* would understand.
Hamid remembered the fine young face under the peaked
Air Force cap. Amman was only forty miles. Why, he was almost there! He could have shouted for sheer excitement.

"Come on, Haryat!" he cried out loud. "We're going to
Amman to see the King."

But where was Haryat? Hamid looked round wildly; then
he began to laugh. Clever Haryat! She had known all along
what was the right thing to do. There she was a hundred
yards or more up the Amman road, nibbling at the lush,
sweet grass. Hamid picked up his handful of bananas and
ran after her.

The River Jordan wound like a green ribbon across the
plain but, after crossing it, the road climbed steeply again
into the Mountains of Moab. It is not easy to gauge walking
speed when going uphill and Hamid wondered how many
miles he had covered. He saw a man waiting by the roadside
with a sheep.

"How much farther is it to Amman?" he asked.

"I don't know the distance. It's an hour by the bus."

"Thank you," said Hamid. The information was not much
help so he trudged on. Half an hour later the bus passed
him and there was the sheep peering through the window,
with the man alongside. Hamid waved and pointed them
out to Haryat.

"I wonder if they would have taken you," he speculated.
Though privately he doubted it. He had never seen a don-
key on the bus that ran between the Damascus Gate and the
Mount of Olives. Or a sheep either, for that matter. But that

was Jerusalem.

"Never mind, we'll be in Amman nearly as soon as the bus," he boasted.

The road up through the hills was a busy one. Haryat shied frequently as the swift cars blasted their horns in warning half a mile behind her and continued until long after they were past. And there were huge Mercedes trucks, grinding up from the Dead Sea with their burden of phosphates to thunder the two hundred miles down the Desert Highway to the port of Aqaba on the Red Sea.

Hamid felt more and more weary as he trudged through the morning. He met no one else to talk to, but he saw a shepherd in the distance, striding at the head of his flock as he led them to fresh pastures. The sun stood almost at its zenith, and still the road climbed ahead of him. Haryat followed obediently, though sometimes Hamid had to stop and give her a tug, for the land was greener here than on the hills round Jerusalem and there was more for her to eat. There were more flowers, too: wild hollyhocks and anchusa and bright blue flax.

"Poor old Haryat," said Hamid at last, slipping an affectionate arm round her neck. "Why shouldn't you have a proper meal while there's plenty of good grass?"

There was a small plantation of fir trees on the opposite side of the road, so he led Haryat across and tied her halter rope to a low branch of one of the trees.

"There," he said. "Now you're safe if any cars startle you."

He propped himself up against the trunk of the fir and started on the bananas. He tossed one of the skins to Haryat but she only sniffed at it disdainfully. That was not her idea of a delicacy. He dropped the other skins by his feet and gazed drowsily across the hills that lay all around. There was wheat growing here, and alfalfa and tobacco. He would tell his father about it when he returned to Jerusalem. Hamid's father's father had worked on the land in those far-away days before he lost his home. Hamid had often heard his father talking about it and of the good things they had to eat in those days.

He jumped up and unpinned Nicky's handkerchief from Haryat's sacking, and came back and spread out his treasures. Why not rest for a while and work on the olive wood? Father Gregory had told him to try to carve something worthwhile.

Even as he picked it up, he remembered something else Father Gregory had told him. "Keep it, but I hope that, whenever you look at it, you will remember where the wood came from."

That was only the day before yesterday and already he had forgotten about the lesson. He had stolen that very morning. Those bananas! There may have been lots of them, but they were not his to take. He kicked savagely at the banana skins. Well, he had done it now. He couldn't *un*-eat the bananas.

He picked up the wood again and looked at the dark brown whorls and wavy lines in the broken ends. What was it telling him to carve? Sometimes, when he held a piece of wood in his hands, it would suggest something to him by its shape; sometimes, as he carved it, the grain would tell him which way to go. He picked up the knife-blade and began to feel his way into the wood.

Presently he sat back and looked at what he had done. "Why!" he cried in surprise. "It's you, Haryat. I do believe it's going to be you."

He worked on, eager and absorbed, for quite a long time, but it was very hot. The bananas had made him feel comfortably full inside. He was tired from walking for so many hours. When he looked up from his work, the shimmer of heat on the tarred road dazzled his eyes, so he closed them.

"I mustn't go to sleep," he told himself. "I have to reach Amman."

But the effort of keeping his eyes open was too much. His lids drooped; his head sank on his breast; within minutes,

Hamid was fast asleep.

The clatter of a big red tractor passing wakened him with a start. He looked with interest at the monster machine, never having seen its like before. He felt refreshed after his rest, though he must have slept longer than he had realized, for the shadows of the firs were lengthening and already the sun was low over the Judaean hills behind him.

He stood up, calling affectionately to Haryat that they must be on their way again. There was no answering whicker, and he spun round to look at the tree to which he had tethered her. There was not a sign of Haryat.

Could she have strayed? He ran to the road and looked anxiously up and down its length but could see no donkey. He scrambled up the slope opposite, but there was no sign of her there either, even though he could see the land rolling for miles to Mount Nebo. Had she wandered deeper into the plantation of fir trees? Hamid dashed back across the road, causing an oncoming car to swerve and its driver to blast a furious rebuke on his horn.

"Haryat! Haryat!" Hamid called.

Silence, except for the roar of the car's engine diminishing in the distance.

Hamid went back to the tree. He was sure he had tied her securely. Absolutely certain. How *could* she have pulled the knot undone?

Then he saw that the knot was still secure on the branch, with two or three inches of rope dangling below it. The rope had been cut. Haryat had been stolen.

Hamid was so stunned with the shock of his discovery that he sat down again. Whatever was he to do? Here he was in the middle of nowhere with no donkey to transport him and no money to pay for a bus, even if there was another one that day. He was too far from Jericho to return there before nightfall and Amman was an unknown number of miles away. He had nothing in the world but a banana, a water bottle and his few small treasures done up in Nicky's hand-kerchief. And there could not be more than another hour or hour and a half of daylight left.

He began to cry then, until he remembered that he was on his way to see the King and the King would not be very impressed with a snivelling cry-baby. He stood up and squared his thin shoulders. He would get to Amman if he had to walk every step of the way. But he did hope that who-ever had taken Haryat would be kind and not beat her. And at the thought of his faithful companion being beaten, he began to cry all over again in big, choking sobs that tore at his breath and made the road go blurred ahead of him.

He strode on manfully and after half an hour came out on the top of a wide plateau. There was less vegetation here, only grey-green camel-thorn casting spiky shadows across earth that glowed copper in the dying light of the sun.

A line of camels appeared over the horizon and moved with slow dignity towards him. The two Bedouin drovers had their *keffiyehs* pulled round their faces. They wore long black robes, kilted up over white trousers, and each carried a rifle slung over his shoulder. Hamid hailed the drovers eagerly.

"Have you seen a donkey, a little white donkey, wearing a necklace with her name on a wooden pendant?"

The drovers laughed at the idea of a donkey wearing a necklace, but they looked grave when they heard she had been stolen.

"And where are you going to, little one, at this hour of the day?" they asked.

"I was on my way to Amman to see the King," replied Hamid. "But . . ." His voice trailed off sadly.

"Come along with us," suggested the drovers. "These camels of ours can move if they have a mind to. We are travelling in the direction of Amman and, who knows, we may even catch up with this Haryat of yours."

Hamid watched apprehensively as one of the drovers grabbed a camel's head-rope and ordered the beast to kneel. It obeyed complainingly, slavering green slime from its disdainful mouth and turning its head to watch Hamid with what, he was sure, was intense dislike. The drover lifted Hamid on the camel's back and climbed up behind him. He showed him how to sit, with right foot tucked under his left knee. It was not too bad while the camel was still.

"*Hat! Hat!*" called the drover, and the camel rose obediently, hind legs first, and then front, in a widly rocking motion that made Hamid cling to its blanket with desperate hands. But the drover's arm was round his waist, and, although it looked a frighteningly long way down to the ground, it was rather fun, once he had become accustomed to the motion. The view was marvellous up there, and the drover was right; a camel could certainly move!

The beast's neck was sticking out at a peculiar angle in front and it was covering the ground with a long, loping gait that seemed fairly to eat up the miles.

They must have travelled for an hour without seeing any other living creature. The rim of the sun was just sliding behind the Judaean hills when they saw a group of gypsies ahead. There were quite a number of them, their donkeys burdened with bundles and kettles and children. Two black goats and a baby kid trotted behind their train. The donkeys were all a uniform brown except one, whose dusty white coat shone rose in the rays of the setting sun.

"Haryat!" shrieked Hamid, almost falling off the camel in his excitement. "Haryat!"

He shouted at the top of his lungs and the rose-colored donkey stopped in its tracks, long ears swivelling like radar scanners.

The camel drover urged his beast forward, unslinging his rifle as he went.

"You're sure it's your donkey, little one?" he demanded.

"Oh yes, indeed it is. See how she answers to her name."
And he called again, "Haryat!"

There was no mistaking the recognition in the way the
donkey turned its head. Even the approaching camels didn't
disturb her.

"Hey, you!" called the drover to the gypsies. "Hand over
that donkey you've stolen."

"Stolen!"

"What donkey?"

"What lies are these?"

A babble of protests arose from the gypsies, and the youth
who was leading Haryat yanked on her rope to urge her forward.

"She's my donkey," protested Hamid shrilly. "You stole
her from me while I was asleep."

"What nonsense is this? Surely you don't believe a child's
chatter?" The gypsies were voluble in their denials. The
drover looked at them uncertainly. The youth took a switch
to Haryat's rump.

"*Imshi, imshi!*" he urged.

Haryat was not to be forced. She remained stubbornly
where she was, legs splayed. The youth struck her again, and
this time, with a quick twist of her behind and a well-timed
kick of her back legs, Haryat sent him sprawling in the dust.
The gypsy bellowed and dropped her leading-rope as he fell.
That gave Haryat her opportunity. She tossed her head and
trotted off the road in the direction of Hamid.

"Look, what did I tell you?" yelled Hamid delightedly.
"You can see her necklace, just as I told you."

That was enough for the drover. He levelled his rifle.

"Be off with you," he called. "And don't let me find you
in this district tomorrow or it will be the worse for you."

The gypsies looked at the levelled rifle and hesitated. They
knew a Bedouin would not miss his shot, so, grumbling
about thieves and brigands, they shambled off along the

highway.

"Filthy scum!" The drover spat with disgust and forced his camel to its knees. Hamid was off its back almost before it had sunk to the ground and was running over the harsh stony ground to his beloved friend.

"Oh, Haryat," he cried, laying his cheek against her dusty neck. "I thought I'd lost you for ever."

The drover watched, smiling, as Haryat nuzzled gently at Hamid's robe, butting him affectionately with her moist nose. "You had better spend tonight at our camp," he said. "Come along, little one. It's not more than half a mile away."

Hamid climbed on Haryat's back and followed the camels. Soon, across the now darkening land, he could faintly discern a gleam of cooking fires.

It was a big camp. There were at least a dozen long, low, open-sided, black tents. Big flocks of sheep and goats and camels had been driven into the hollow where the camp was pitched. Dogs started snapping and barking as Hamid and his companions approached, but one of the drovers called to them and their threatening growls changed to yelps of pleasure. A small girl staggered past, nursing a baby kid nearly as big as herself, and stopped to stare curiously at Hamid and Haryat.

One drover saw to the camels and made sure that Haryat was fed and watered; the other, with an affectionate arm on Hamid's shoulder, took him across to his father's tent and recounted the story of their meeting.

Sheikh Mansour was an old man, his face seamed with the harshness of seventy years in the desert. His nose jutted in a proud beak above the full, white moustache, but the eyes above were gentle.

"*Ahlan wa sahlan!*" he said in courteous greeting. "You are indeed welcome."

He was reclining on one elbow on a colorful rug that had

been spread on the bare earth. Cushions of silk and velvet were piled in casual confusion. In the entrance to the tent several brass coffee-pots with spouts like the crescent moon steamed invitingly over a low fire of camel dung.

Hamid sat nervously on the cushion to which he had been waved and wondered what would happen next. There were other men sitting round on the rug, some of them smoking. Two of them wore the red-and-white-checked *hatta* and cartridge-studded bandoliers of Camel Corps men. From the other side of a curtain that divided the tent, he could hear feminine giggles. Presumably the sheikh's womenfolk were there. Hamid half wished he could be on that side of the curtain. He wanted his mother very badly. Then he pulled himself together. Those were baby thoughts. He was being treated like a man and an honored guest. He forced his attention back to his host and tried to understand the grown-up conversation.

The sheikh poured a little coffee into a handleless cup and passed it to him. It was strong, black, and bitter, and flavored with cardamom—not a bit like the syrupy-sweet Turkish coffee of Jerusalem. Hamid watched the other men to see what they did. Then, copying their example, he drained the cup and held it out for more as courtesy demanded.

The coffee-drinking went on seemingly for hours. Hamid shivered a little in the cold evening air and wondered if he had missed the evening meal. It seemed a long, long time since his midday banana. He felt as if the front of his stomach were touching his back, he was so empty.

The conversation droned on, the coffee-pot circulated again and again, and still there was no sign of food. Hamid gave up trying to follow the thread of the discussion and instead covertly studied his surroundings.

There was a big brass bedstead in one corner of the tent, heaped with more cushions and covered with a beautiful coverlet of rich brocade. By the side of the bed stood a very modern transistor radio. The sheikh leaned across and switched it on for the news from Radio Amman. Hamid listened, fascinated. He had heard radios in the shops in Jerusalem, of course, but he had not been so close to one before.

There was a lot that Hamid did not understand, about countries that were only names to him. And something about taxes. And then Hamid listened eagerly as the announcer described a visit by the King to inaugurate a new irrigation scheme in the north of Jordan. He went on to talk about the weather and the sheikh switched off the set.

Hamid gazed out through the tent-opening into the night. He wondered what an "irrigation scheme" was and whether he dared ask his host.

But the thought died almost as it was born, for at that moment his friends the two drovers staggered into the tent, bearing between them a vast platter piled high with steaming rice and boiled lamb. It was *mensaf*, the traditional food offered by a Bedouin to his guests.

Hamid thought he had never seen anything quite so wonderful. The meat gleamed golden and moist under the lamplight, and the savory smell of it made the juices run in his mouth so fast that he had to swallow. Conversation ceased as each man rolled back his sleeve and reached out his right hand to select a portion from the dish. Hamid followed suit. The meat was hot to hold, but he tore at it hungrily. He savored it, warm and succulent, all the way down into his inside.

He tried to manage the rice as well, watching how the men rolled a small portion into a ball in the one hand they were using and then popped it into their mouths with a neat flick of the wrist. Hamid had never had time to practice the niceties of eating. At home it was a case of pushing down as much as possible of what was available in the shortest time. He got in a bit of a mess with the rice, but nobody seemed to notice. He ate and ate until his stomach was tight as a drum.

He had never eaten so much in all his life—not ever. It was wonderful.

What with the food and the warmth of the crowded tent and the lateness of the hour, fumes of sleep engulfed him. Long before the ceremonial handwashing that followed the *mensaf*, Hamid had keeled over in his place and fallen fast asleep.

He was vaguely aware of strong arms lifting him, of a soft pillow beneath his head and a warm rug being tucked round his weary frame. Then oblivion descended.

Outside, an immensity of stars wheeled in their courses round the heavens. All the camp was in darkness, save for the small glow of the fires.

Somewhere in the distance a jackal called, and one of the camels stirred and shifted in its sleep. A breath of wind stirred the tent flaps and whispered through the dry camel-thorn. But Hamid heard none of this: he slept.

Chapter Nine

To See the King

Amman, like Rome, is built on seven hills. Its old name was Philadelphia, and it was one of the ten Greek cities beyond Jordan that together were known as the Decapolis. But to Hamid, seeing it for the first time on that Thursday morning, it was as modern as Sheikh Mansour's transistor radio.

It had been an altogether wonderful morning. The Bedouin had been so kind and generous. Hamid had breakfasted off *laban* and freshly baked bread. He had been furnished with a supply of bread and cheese for his journey that day. In addition, Hamid's friend the camel-drover had found an old *agal* of black woolen rope to hold his tattered *keffiyeh* in place, so he felt now that he looked a true son of the desert, instead of an urchin of the Jerusalem streets.

The drover took him part of the way to Amman on one of the camels, with Haryat trotting briskly behind. So when Hamid at last bade a grateful goodbye to his friends and set off alone, he was only five miles from the capital.

He hadn't realized that any part of Jordan, apart from Jericho, could be so green and fertile. There were nurseries of young trees and acres of corn and tobacco. There were tractors and garages and a constant stream of cars. The five miles seemed no distance at all, there were so many new things to see and admire.

So here he was, trotting expectantly down a wide, tree-lined boulevard, wondering which of the elegant flower-clad villas could be the King's palace. One of them surely must be; ordinary people could not live in such splendid houses.

He stopped and peered over the wall of one of them. A gardener was watering the red soil under the roses and hibiscus bushes.

"As-salaam alaykum," said Hamid courteously. "Can you tell me which of these buildings is the King's palace?"

The man set down the hose and came across to him. "These houses the King's palace! You're a long way out of your way, boy."

Hamid's face fell. "This is Amman?" he asked. "This is where the King lives?"

The man nodded and came out through the gate. "You want to continue on down this road," he said, pointing. "Keep going till you come to the city center. You can't miss it. There's the Omari mosque and the Continental Hotel close together."

"The Omari mosque and the Continental Hotel," repeated Hamid.

"Go on past the mosque until you come to the Roman amphitheatre. There's no mistaking that. It's right on the main road and it's huge. The road leads on from there past the Tomb of the Unknown Warrior and up to the Basman Palace. Are you going to watch the changing of the guard?"

"I'm going to see the King," said Hamid importantly.

The gardener laughed. "I'm sure the King will be glad to see you and your donkey."

Still chuckling, he went back to his watering. Hamid set off down the road, reassured. The man had said the King would be pleased to see him and Haryat.

It was not very comfortable for Haryat in Amman. There were too many cars, and the constant blare of horns made her uneasy. Hamid led her the rest of the way, holding tightly on to her halter. Poor Haryat! She was tugged this way and that as Hamid's eye was caught first by one shop and then by another. He forgot he was dragging Haryat after him when he darted across the footpath to gaze at the opulent window displays, whether of sleek, gleaming cars or elegant Western clothes.

He found the Roman amphitheatre without difficulty. There was an arcade of tall columns along the main road, and a half-circle of what seemed to be seats, rising in tiers up the hillside, and a great big arena. There were tourists everywhere, strolling across the arena, sitting on the seats and climbing up to the top of the tiers to see the view. Roman, the gardener had said it was. Hamid wondered what the Romans had used it for. They certainly got around.

He continued along the road as the gardener had instructed him, passed the Tomb of the Unknown Warrior and so found himself at the entrance to the palace grounds.

Hamid had been so occupied in his mind with the hope that the King was going to straighten out all his troubles that he had not stopped to consider how one approached a king. The first obstacle he encountered was the guard on the palace gate.

The Basman Palace stands on a hill on the eastern side of Amman. It is approached by a long, winding drive, at the foot of which is a control post and a uniformed sentry. Hamid led Haryat across the wide road opposite the control post and stopped to admire the sentry.

The sentry stood as motionless as a carved figure, his body as rigid as the rifle by his side. Only the dark-brown, watchful eyes betrayed any sign of life. His red-and-white, betasselled *hatta* was tossed back arrogantly over his shoulder. The black *agal* was tipped at a rakish angle over one eye. He was so still he surely could not be real!

"Heh! You!" His sudden shout pulled Hamid up short as he made to lead Haryat up the palace approach.

"What? Me?" Hamid turned back.

"Where do you think you're going with that donkey?"

"I'm going to see the King," replied Hamid importantly.

"Oh no, you're not," said the sentry. "We can't have

every scruffy little urchin in the country barging in here.
Be off with you."

Hamid stood his ground. "I must see the King. It's important."

"And I suppose it's important that that donkey sees the
King as well, eh?" queried the sentry, with heavy sarcasm
which was quite lost on Hamid.

"Haryat goes everywhere with me," he said. "She's my
best friend."

The sentry burst out laughing at that, a laugh that was
instantly checked as his sergeant came across.

"What's going on here? Move this lad on. He's blocking
the traffic."

Sure enough, two sleek cars were waiting to pass into the
drive. Hamid tugged Haryat to one side and the cars went
through, smartly saluted by the sergeant and the sentry.

"You heard," said the sergeant to Hamid, relaxing again.
"Go on, *imshi!*"

"Please!" implored Hamid. "I *must* see the King. I'll
leave Haryat with you, if you say so."

"I'm not warning you again," said the sergeant. "Go on.
Move!"

Hamid appeared to hesitate and the sergeant took a step
towards him. At that very instant, Hamid, who had been
undoing the safety-pin that secured Nicky's handkerchief to
the sacking, thrust the pin deep into Haryat's rear. With a
wild toss of the head, Haryat bounded forward past the
sentry and up the drive. Hamid remained just where he was,
looking innocent.

The sergeant fumed. "Get that donkey out of here," he
yelled.

Hamid beamed. "Okay!" he said, and scurried after Haryat up the drive. He had to run all the way up to and round
the first bend before he caught her.

"Good, Haryat," said Hamid, patting her affectionately.

"You did that very well. I hope I didn't hurt you."

Haryat slowed down at the sound of the familiar voice, and Hamid was able to take hold of her halter again. He looked round him eagerly.

There were roses everywhere, great fragrant beds of them, freshly watered. They looked so fresh and clean that Hamid became aware of his own dirty appearance. He hastily spat on his hands and tried to wipe them clean on his *djubah*. He took off his *keffiyeh* and scrubbed at his face with a corner of it. That was a bit better.

He thought he could hear the sentry's boots as he pounded up the drive after him, so he hurriedly mounted Haryat and urged her briskly up the rest of the drive. They came out at last at the foot of a long flight of steps, flanked by stone lions, that led up to the main doors of the palace. There were two more sentries on duty at the foot of the steps. They looked a trifle startled to see a disreputable-looking boy and a donkey at the very entrance to the palace.

"You can't take that donkey into the palace, you know," muttered one of the sentries out of the corner of his mouth, while still standing rigidly in front of his sentry-box.

"Oh, dear," said Hamid. "Where can I leave her? Can you hold her for me while I see the King?"

He looped the halter over the surprised sentry's rifle and ran up the steps. The sentry shouted to him to stop, but he was climbing up the steps two at a time and the sentry did not quite know what to do, encumbered as he was with Haryat. If he let the donkey go, who knew what damage she might not do to the King's roses!

Hamid paused at the open entrance. The doors were very big. Did one knock or just go inside?

Before he could do either, his view was blocked by the hilt of a big, curving, silver sword just about level with his eyes. He followed the sword down to the full skirt of a long coat over high, gleaming boots. Startled, he looked back from the boots up the coat to a handsome, white-moustachioed face under a tall Cossack hat.

"And *what*, might I ask, young man," demanded White Moustache, "are you doing at the palace?"

"If you please, *sayed*," said Hamid, "I've come to see the King. It's very important," he added. "I've come all the way from Jerusalem."

"That's a long way for a child," said White Moustache. "Did you come by car?"

"Oh no," replied Hamid. "I came on Haryat." He pointed back down the steps to where the donkey, straining to reach the rose beds, was engaged in a tug-of-war with the scarlet-faced sentry.

White Moustache, who was one of the King's Circassian bodyguard, lifted a faintly surprised eyebrow. "Indeed?" he said. "And what is your business with the King?"

Hamid's eyes dropped. "I'd rather not say," he muttered. "I don't want anyone to know except the King."

The Circassian's moustache did not even twitch. "I'm afraid you've come on the wrong day," he said courteously, as if small boys who had private business with the King were an everyday occurrence. "His Majesty is not in Amman at present. But he will be in the palace on Monday. He would grant you an audience then. He is always available to his people on Mondays."

"Not until Monday!" Hamid's face crumpled. "But I have to be in Jerusalem on Monday! Will he be back today? Could I wait?"

"I'm sorry," said the Circassian guard firmly. "No audiences until Monday."

Hamid was stunned. It just could not happen like this. To have come all this way and yet not see the King! His small figure seemed to become even smaller. Mechanically he descended the steps, mechanically he accepted Haryat's halter from the sentry, mechanically he trailed past the rose beds back down the long, winding drive.

The first sentry was waiting for him halfway down.

"So you've caught your donkey at last . . . ," he began, but Hamid walked past him without a word or a glance, out of the palace grounds, across the wide road and back to the Roman amphitheatre. When he reached the ruins, he sat down on the first row of seats and let the tears flow unchecked. Haryat blew down his neck and butted her soft nose gently into his shoulder.

Hamid wiped his nose on his sleeve and stroked Haryat absently. He gazed round him at the Roman ruins and suddenly hated them.

"I should have remembered, Haryat," he said—and there was all the disillusion of a shattered dream in his voice. "Father Gregory never told me the end of the story. He said how that man Paul went to Rome—but he never said whether he actually *saw* Caesar or not."

CHAPTER TEN

The Price of Friendship

THERE was nothing to be gained from sitting moping in the middle of Amman. Taking stock of his position, Hamid realized he was in dire difficulty.

He had to appear in court on Monday and he was three days' journey away from Jerusalem. He had enough food for today but none for the days ahead. He had no money at all and he could hardly count on meeting a friendly Bedouin this time. In fact, after this morning's disaster, he didn't feel he could count on his luck any more.

The important thing was to obtain some money. He undid Nicky's handkerchief and spread out his possessions on the seat beside him. The two marbles and the colored pebble were of no value, so he set those on one side. There remained the Roman tile, the carved lizard and the likeness of Haryat that he was fashioning from the olive wood. Should he sell the tile? There were plenty of tourists about who might be interested, and he was sick of the Romans anyway.

And yet . . . He could see Father Gregory's strong, brown hands holding the tile, could hear his warm, vibrant voice as he told him about the siege of Jerusalem. No, he could not part with the tile. It would be like . . . like . . . selling part of Father Gregory. You did not sell your friends. And, though everything seemed to be going wrong despite what Father Gregory had said, Hamid still thought of him as his friend.

As his mind went back to the sunlit Garden he felt again

its peace, and he reached out almost absently, picked up his knife and the olive wood and began to carve. Using one's hands was soothing. There was no hurry any more. He could take time to carve. Monday would bring what it had to bring. *Insh 'Allah.*

Slowly the little figure grew under his hands. The wood seemed almost to guide him. It was going to be a good donkey, Hamid could see that already. This was no staring-eyed, clumsy-footed, mass-produced donkey from the *souq.* This was Haryat herself, with her long expressive ears and gentle, long-lashed eyes and dainty hooves. The very grain of the wood highlighted the plane of cheek and flank. He worked on, absorbed.

A shadow fell across Hamid's feet, and he looked up to see a small group of tourists watching him with interest. He smiled shyly and bent to his task again.

"That sure is clever carving, little boy," said one of the tourists. They must be American, Hamid decided. He scrambled to his feet.

"Thank you," he said. Then, proudly, "Look, I carve Haryat."

"My, isn't that just too cute!" The American's wife joined in. "Do you want to sell it, little boy?"

"Oh no!" Hamid clutched the precious carving to him. It was too special to part with. What could he say?

"Not finished," he said. "You like lizard?" he added, stooping swiftly to pick it up and offer it to them. "Fifty fils," he offered. "I, Hamid, make it."

"No, I don't like lizards," said the American lady. "They make me think of snakes. It's the donkey I like."

But Hamid shook his head.

"What's this?" asked the American man. He was poking with his stick at the Roman tile laid out on the handkerchief.

"Oh, take care," cried Hamid. "That tile is very old,

worth plenty money. Romans make that tile at Jerusalem."

"Is that so?" drawled the American. "Then how come it's turned up in Amman?"

"I come from Jerusalem," said Hamid. "I go there now."

"I'll give you two hundred fils for that tile," said the American.

Hamid gasped. It sounded a princely sum. He looked up swiftly and saw the glint of desire behind the rimless glasses.

"It's . . . it's . . . not for sale," he said hastily.

"As you like," replied the American. "But think about it, and if you change your mind we're staying at the Philadelphia Hotel just opposite here. Welburn's the name. Hiram G. Welburn."

Hamid watched them go. He did not know why he had refused to sell the tile. He needed the money badly enough. Equally, he could have parted with the carved donkey. But the words burned in his mind. *Keep it*, Father Gregory had said. *Keep it, and carve something special.*

It was wonderful, however, that people should think he carved well enough to want to buy his work. In the end, he managed to sell the lizard for forty fils. It was not much, thought Hamid, when he reflected that the mass-produced donkeys in the *souq* sold for two or three hundred fils apiece; but if he spent the money carefully, he might just manage for food. He would not need much and he did not have to pay anything for Haryat. But he would not spend his forty fils in Amman, he decided. The shops were altogether too splendid. He would see what he could find in one of the villages. He wrapped up the tile and the carving again and, with a last glance round the vast Roman amphitheatre, set out again for home, back past the Omari mosque and the Continental Hotel, back down the long, tree-lined boulevard where he had talked to the gardener—was it only a few hours ago?

He had intended trying to cover as much ground as possible before nightfall, but it was much more tiring to walk through the streets of a big busy city, with the noise and the petrol fumes and the rush of traffic, than ever it had been, climbing up through the Mountains of Moab. And Haryat did not like the traffic either; it seemed to upset her. So Hamid decided to sit down, once they were clear of the city, and have a rest. There was a plantation of trees by the roadside, that looked cool and inviting. It occurred to Hamid that, if he and Haryat rested now in the hot afternoon, they might walk on by starlight, when it was cooler. He could not miss the road.

He tied Haryat's halter to the post of a barbed-wire fence that surrounded the plantation, ducked under the strands himself and was soon fast asleep under the trees. Haryat cropped nervously at the grass by the roadside. She shied at each car that tore past.

Hamid never knew whether it was the splutter of the combine or some sound from Haryat that broke in on his dream. He came to with a start. Haryat was in trouble. That was what he had been dreaming.

He scrambled to his feet, knuckling the sleep from his eyes, as the huge combine harvester clattered past. But it was not a dream. Haryat was caught up on the wire. In backing away from the monster machine, she had somehow wound herself tight in the halter and was now struggling frantically to free herself.

"Oh wait, Haryat! Keep still!" Hamid rushed to her side, seeking with words and hands to calm the panic-stricken animal.

He managed to hold her head, and she became steadier. She stood shivering while Hamid pulled loose the ugly strand of wire that was caught in her chest. Her white coat was stained an ugly brown where the cut had bled, and even as Hamid looked a fresh blob of scarlet welled up from the wound and trickled down the matted fur.

Hamid tugged the *keffiyeh* from his head and tried to staunch the wound. But how did one bandage a donkey?

"Don't die, Haryat," he begged. "*Please* don't die."

He stood uncertainly by the roadside. Ought he to take Haryat to a hospital? Did hospitals admit donkeys? Two days ago, he had almost fled when he saw a mounted policeman, but now, as he saw one trotting up the road, he ran to meet him.

"Please, can you help?" he begged, as the policeman drew rein beside him. "It's Haryat. She's hurt."

"Where is she?" The policeman dismounted and looked round him.

"*Here*," said Hamid impatiently. "Haryat. She's my donkey."

The policeman laughed at that and pulled the corners of his yellow *keffiyeh* from round his face, tossing them back over his shoulders. But his face was grave as he examined Haryat's injury.

"You must take her to a vet," he declared. "That wound needs stitching."

"To a vet?" asked Hamid. "I don't understand."

"A doctor who looks especially after animals. Here,"— he pulled out his notebook and scribbled down a name— "that's the nearest one. In Amman. He's on the outskirts of the town."

Amman! It meant going back. Still, Hamid could not desert Haryat now. He thanked the policeman and set off, back the way he had come.

The policeman watched him go, concerned at Hamid's distress over his donkey. It touched a chord in his memory. Someone had reported a missing boy in Jerusalem. There was something about a donkey, too. Could there be any connection? But he dismissed the idea. Jerusalem was miles away. No child could do that journey through the wilderness. It could not be this boy.

Hamid found the veterinary surgeon's place with some difficulty. *Ahmed Hatar*, said the name-plate on the door. Hamid's nose wrinkled as he went in. There was a funny smell about the place—a bit like when Father Gregory had dressed his father's foot, only more so. Everything was very shiny and clean. Mr Hatar himself was shiny and clean, too, in a spotless white coat.

He was kind and sympathetic and clucked over Haryat in a way no one had ever talked about her before. "Nasty cut. Nasty," he said.

Haryat didn't back away when he touched her. She stood quite still, as if she understood that he was trying to help. Only her ears, lying back along her head, and her rolling eyeballs showed that she was nervous.

"Hm," said Mr Hatar. "The cut will have to be stitched. Barbed wire, you said? She'd better have an anti-tetanus injection as well."

He talked on as he busied himself laying out instruments

and sutures. Hamid did not understand a word of it, but he watched anxiously, dark eyes following every move.

The vet picked up a syringe with a long needle. "Just hold her steady," he said, and before Hamid could protest, he had pinched up some flesh on Haryat's neck and plunged in the needle of the syringe—much farther than Hamid had stuck the safety pin.

"What did you do that for!" protested Hamid indignantly, momentarily stunned out of his shyness as he felt Haryat flinch.

"That was what we call a tranquillizer," explained Mr Hatar, preparing another syringe. "It calms her down so that she won't worry about what I do next to her. I'm giving her a local anaesthetic now, so that she won't feel anything at all while I stitch up the cut. See—here in the area surrounding the wound." Once again he thrust the needle home. It was Hamid who winced that time. "Now for the stitches."

Hamid had had an imaginary picture of Mr Hatar using a needle and thread as he had seen the girls doing in Miss Yvonne Salamon's refugee shop in Jerusalem—making tiny embroidery stitches with fine needles and colored silks, putting beautiful designs on handkerchiefs and table linen. It was quite a relief to see him make two quick loops with some coarse-looking thread and fasten them off with knots. His fingers were every bit as deft and neat as the girls', and Haryat had not even twitched an ear.

"Is that all?" asked Hamid.

"That's all," said Mr Hatar. "The wound should heal quite cleanly now. If you bring her back next week, I will take the stitches out. Now, I'll just give her the anti-tetanus injection."

Hamid scarcely noticed as the fresh injection was put into Haryat's shoulder. "Bring her back next week?" he said in dismay. "But I can't do that. I live in Jerusalem."

"That's all right," said Mr Hatar, unperturbed. "Just take her to the vet in Jerusalem. He will take the stitches out for you. In that case, you'd better pay me now. That will be two *dinars*."

"Two dinars!" Hamid's face blanched with dismay. "I . . . I . . . didn't think there'd be anything to pay. I've only got forty fils."

Two dinars! He had never had so much money ever in his life. He doubted whether his father had.

Mr Hatar looked at him sternly. "You surely must have realized that you can't expect medical treatment for nothing. Do you know someone who could lend you the money?"

Hamid shook his head. He could not speak.

"Then I'm afraid you must leave your donkey here until you do find the money," said Mr Hatar crisply. "I'm sorry, but drugs cost money. And I have to live, you know."

He led Haryat out through another door into a sort of yard. After a minute or two he came back. Hamid was still standing in the room. He had not moved.

"Run along, boy." Then, more kindly, he added, "Your donkey will be all right. I won't hurt her. Just bring me the two dinars and you shall have her back."

Hamid stepped out into the street and looked round him despairingly. There was nobody about and, even if there were, how could he stop them and ask for two dinars? Two piastres, perhaps, but not two dinars. Anyway, he had always hated begging—and if any of the tourist police caught him begging he would be deep in trouble again.

He trudged aimlessly along the pavement. He had to pay Mr Hatar somehow. Without his skill, Haryat might have died. And he could not desert Haryat now. Why, if it had not been for Haryat, he would never have reached Amman, or met the Bedouins, or reached the Basman Palace, whether the King was there or not. Haryat was his friend. She was even the model for his carving. . . . The carving was the answer!

He paused on the pavement as he worked it out in his mind. He could carve another model, but he could not get another Haryat from anywhere. He would seek out Mr Welburn at the Philadelphia Hotel and ask him to buy the olive-wood carving for two dinars.

The Welburns were sitting in the garden outside the Philadelphia Hotel with some friends, sipping long, delicious-looking iced drinks out of tall glasses. Cigarette smoke curled up, blue and lazy, in the stillness of the late afternoon.

At least there was no problem in entering the hotel. Hamid waited until the commissionaire had gone inside and then slipped through the gate into the garden.

"Mr Welburn," he whispered.

"Well, well," drawled the American. "Look, honey. Here's that Arab boy again."

"Please, *sayed*," said Hamid. "I sell the donkey."

He unwrapped the handkerchief and set the little carving on the table. It was no bigger than one of the tall glasses.

"Now isn't that just too bad," exclaimed the American lady. "I've already bought another one. You know, it's not nearly as good as yours."

She reached into a bag at her side and took out a tissue-wrapped parcel. When she had unwrapped the layers of paper and set her own donkey beside Hamid's, he could feel, even through his dreadful disappointment, a surge of pride at the difference in the workmanship. But he had urgent matters to settle.

"You like the tile, *sayed*?" Hamid turned to Mr Welburn. "I must have two dinars today.My donkey, she sick. Please, *sayed*. Two dinars for tile?"

"Two dinars! That's two thousand fils! I offered you two hundred," said the American. "It's probably a fake anyway."

"No, truly, *sayed*. Father Gregory at Gethsemane, he say

the tile genuine Roman."

"Let me see the tile." One of the American's companions, a thin, elderly gentleman with a fringe of white hair round his balding pate, reached out and picked up the tile. He peered at it through narrowed eyes and then produced a pair of spectacles from his pocket and put them on. He studied the tile again.

"How did you come by this, boy?" he asked Hamid.

"I find the tile on Mount of Olives. Father Gregory, he say the tile genuine Roman. Made by Tenth Legion," he added proudly. The elderly gentleman nodded.

"The lad's right," he said to the American. "See the badge of the Fretensis—the galley and the boar."

"You don't say!" said the American. "It really is genuine, professor?"

"I'll stake my reputation on it," replied the elderly gentleman. He turned to Hamid. "I'll give you two dinars for the tile, boy."

Suiting his action to the words, he took out his wallet, extracted two crisp bank-notes and handed them to Hamid.

"I'll check it with the Department of Antiquities over the road in the morning, but I've no doubt in my mind that it's genuine," he said. "No doubt whatever."

Hamid did not wait to hear any more. With a hurried "*Shookran*" to the professor, he gathered up the olive-wood carving and, clutching the bank-notes tightly in his fist, ran from the garden of the hotel before the customer could change his mind.

Haryat was saved. Allah be praised, he had two whole dinars to redeem her. And, what was more, how pleased Father Gregory would be: the two dinars had been come by honestly.

CHAPTER ELEVEN

The Way to the Inn

THEY would have been all right if it had not been for the *khamsin*. It began on Friday as a riffle of south-east wind that bowed the fields of barley outside Amman into tossing seas of gold. But it brought no freshness of the ocean with it, for it was a hot wind, blowing across from the deserts of Arabia. The sky was white with heat. Hamid urged Haryat on anxiously. He knew that wind; he knew that, as its name suggested, it would blow for fifty days before it spent itself.

By Saturday it was whipping up the dust between the camel-thorn on the Mountains of Moab. Hamid wound the *keffiyeh* round his mouth to keep out the dust and tucked the corners into the *agal*. The air was hot and dry, the earth parched. He had managed to fill the water bottle, but he was worried about water for Haryat.

As he came over the hills to the Jordan plain, he should have been able to see the tower of the Augusta Victoria hospital on the top of the Mount of Olives like a guiding beacon on the skyline, to lead him the last twenty-odd miles home. But the Jordan plain danced in a quiver of heat below him, and the hills of Judea were scarcely visible. The Dead Sea lay like a burnished mirror: a burning white sea reflecting a burning white sky.

The whitened drums that marked the edge of the road stood in pools of water that shimmered on the macadam. Hamid urged Haryat forward, only to find that the pools receded, to reappear a few yards further on.

His face was caked with dust, his eyes narrowed against

the glare. He stopped to wet his lips from the water-bottle and surveyed Haryat anxiously. Her ears hung down, and she kept turning her head as the wind drove sideways into her face.

"Keep going, Haryat," he urged. "We'll come to water soon."

It was growing dusk as they reached the Hussein Bridge over the River Jordan. The water level was low, and the river trickled sluggishly between the high, red, earth banks. Hamid scrambled down to the water's edge, slipping and slithering down the steep slope. Haryat picked her way down more cautiously and thrust her nose gratefully into the water. Hamid knelt at the edge and splashed water over his face and neck, reckless of his clothes. Then he waded into the water and splashed it over Haryat as well, so that her dusty white coat was streaked with runnels of red-brown mud. Her ears pricked as the life-giving water revived her. Hamid refilled the water bottle, and then the pair of them scrambled back up the bank and set off across the bridge.

Over to the left, the lights of the Dead Sea Hotel and Casino sprang into life. *The Lowest Spot on Earth*: that was what it said on the huge sign that advertised the hotel. One thousand, two hundred and fifty feet below sea level. Was that what he had learned at school? Hamid was too tired to remember.

At least the lights were some indication of life in this awful place. Hamid thought he had never seen anything so dreadful as the next mile of road. Great humps and hillocks reared up on either side, white with salt, sterile and sinister as some imagined moonscape.

The wind strengthened and moaned round the hummocks. Hamid shivered, despite the heat of this vast crack in the earth's surface. Haryat shied at every shadow.

He had better rest. The wilderness lay ahead between here and Jerusalem and there was no other road. Better to tackle that in the daylight.

He passed a big flood-lit advertisement for some airline. A great jet streamed across the sign, like the air liners Hamid had seen coming in low to land at Jerusalem Airport. With one of those he could be home in five minutes!

Home! Even the prospect of court on Monday could not diminish the pleasure with which Hamid thought of the little shack on the Mount of Olives. He thought of his mother and father and Ferial. Then he began to feel guilty. He had not told them where he was going. How much worry had he caused them? He had been away a whole week.

Big tears of shame and misery and fatigue began to slide over his cheeks. He sat down by the roadside and pulled Haryat down beside him.

"I'll make it up to them, Haryat. I will indeed," he promised, snuggling up against her warm, furry side. She turned her head and nuzzled him gently.

Thank goodness, it was warm here near the Dead Sea, even though the sun was down. The last two nights had been bitterly cold. Amman, like Jerusalem, is two thousand five hundred feet above sea level and in his thin robe Hamid had slept only fitfully under the stars. He did not sleep well even now, for he was very hungry. He had not eaten at all that day. The forty fils had all gone the day before.

He woke unrefreshed on Sunday morning. He felt dizzy, shivery and sick. He drank some water and then he *was* sick, and for a little while he felt better. The wind was stronger than ever, bringing with it stinging clouds of sand that gritted his eyes and teeth.

Haryat had moved a little way off in search of food, but she came when he called. "Can you carry me today, Haryat?" he asked, heaving himself wearily on to her back. Haryat flicked an ear and moved on slowly as he dug his heels into her side.

After some time, they passed the turning where the road branched off to Jericho and plodded on up the long, steep, winding road to Jerusalem. Before long the heat was stifling. It dazzled off the rocks and the road. The sand-laden wind lashed them. Cars and trucks ground up the hill, overtook them and passed on, choking them with dust and exhaust fumes.

Hamid swayed on Haryat's back. His ears were singing. His eyes hurt. His tongue felt like sandpaper. But he had to go on. He had to be in court tomorrow. Just another few miles. Just another few hours. If only the road were not uphill all the way!

He had lost all control of Haryat now. She picked her own way up the hill, and Hamid did not notice when she strayed into one of the loops of the old, narrow, twisting road that the new, broad highway had replaced.

Hamid jerked back to consciousness as Haryat stumbled on the loose stones. "We're going the wrong way, Haryat," he murmured, sliding off her to walk her back to the road.

But the stony ground tilted to meet him. The sky and the sun and the rocks spun into a dizzy kaleidoscope. His legs buckled beneath him and he lay still.

Haryat nosed uncertainly at his prostrate form; then she wandered back to the highway.

Mrs. Bourne and Nicky relaxed in the front seat of the big Buick. Mr. Bourne put his foot down on the accelerator as he began the steep run up to Jerusalem from the Dead Sea.

It had been a wonderful week. They had seen the caves at Qmran where the Dead Sea scrolls were found; they had examined the excavations of the ancient walls of Jericho and seen the vast ruins of Jerash in the hills beyond Amman. They had crossed the desert to the hidden city of Petra and ridden on horseback through the narrow defile that had cut off the rock-hewn city from the outside world for centuries. From there they had driven to Aqaba on the

Red Sea, where they had lazed on the sun-drenched beaches and dived through the clear green water to look at the beautiful coral gardens. Now, sated with sun and scenery, they were on their way back to Jerusalem and the Astor Hotel. There would be one last day of sight-seeing and present-buying, and then, on Tuesday, Nicky and his mother would fly back from Jerusalem to Beirut and from there to London for the beginning of the summer term. Mr. Bourne would return south to his job as an engineer, working on the Hejaz railway, extending the line that ran from Damascus to Ma'an so that it would eventually carry on down to Medina.

"We'll soon be up to the Inn of the Good Samaritan," said Mr. Bourne. "What a pity you haven't got your camera, Nicky. It would make an interesting picture to show at school."

"I do hope the police have found it," replied Nicky. "There were some extra special shots on the film. I'll never be able to take them again—unless Mummy and I fly out next year?" he added hopefully.

"What's going on ahead?" said Mr. Bourne, ignoring Nicky's hint.

Quite a line of traffic had formed, both up and down the hill, and there was a furious argument in progress on car-horns.

"There's a donkey wandering in the road," said Mrs. Bourne. "It's holding up the traffic."

"Surely the road's wide enough for cars to get round it. There's room for a whole herd of donkeys," protested her husband. "I did want to get a good run up the hill. Now I shall have to grind up in bottom gear all the way."

The car inched forward.

"It's more than just the donkey," said Mrs. Bourne, craning forward in her seat. "Can you see, Nicky?"

"There's a rock-fall. It's blocking half the road."

"Yes—that and the donkey together have reduced the traffic to single file," added his mother.

Mr. Bourne switched off the ignition while the descending stream of cars came past. At last it was their turn to move again. Mr. Bourne let in the clutch and started on up the hill.

Suddenly he jammed his foot on the brake so hard that the two passengers shot off the seat. The donkey had sat down in the middle of the only clear lane of the road.

"Drat the beast!" fumed Mr. Bourne, as a furious fanfare of horns started from the line of vehicles behind him. "What do they expect me to do—run over it?"

He blew his horn repeatedly, but the donkey only put its head down and laid its ears flat.

"Poor thing!" exclaimed Mrs. Bourne. "It's probably terrified."

"Terrified, my foot! It's just plain stubborn," muttered her husband, blasting the horn again.

"Look, dear," said Mrs. Bourne. "That isn't going to help. Someone will have to move the creature, otherwise it will cause a bad accident."

"I know," sighed her husband. "That somebody will have to be me. Come on, Nicky. Let's get it over." He climbed out of the car. "You drive on past the obstruction, my dear, and pull in at the first opportunity. We'll walk on up as soon as we've shifted this animal."

Mrs. Bourne moved over to the driving-seat.

"Give me Trafalgar Square any day," muttered Mr. Bourne, as he and Nicky approached the donkey. "At least the pigeons fly!"

He gave the prostrate donkey a slap on the rump. "Come up, you stupid animal," he said.

The donkey stayed where it was.

"It's got a halter. Shall I pull while you push?" suggested Nicky.

"All right."

Nicky took hold of the rope. "Ready?"

"Okay. *Heave!*"

But no matter how hard Nicky pulled nor how force-fully Mr. Bourne pushed from behind, the donkey stayed where it was. It sat back on its hind legs, front legs splayed and neck extended.

An Arab driver joined them. "*Imshi! Imshi!*" he said to the donkey, but it only let one ear droop and didn't move.

They stood back, baffled. Nicky let go of the halter and the donkey shook its head vigorously. Something round its neck moved with the vibration.

"Daddy, look at that necklace thing round its neck. Surely it's the donkey that used to see by the hotel on the Mount of Olives."

Mr. Bourne reached out a hand to examine the piece of wood that hung from the donkey's neck. "It's got Arabic writing on it," he said. "H-A-R-Y-A-T," he spelt out slowly. "Haryat."

It worked like a charm. At the sound of the name, the donkey rose to its feet and allowed itself to be moved out of the way, clearing the road. Mrs. Bourne drove past with a cheery toot of the horn and the now big jam of traffic began to sort itself out.

"Now what do we do?" asked Mr. Bourne. "Haryat! Maybe it's the animal's name?" He laughed. "Just look at the silly thing, Nicky. You'd honestly think she was trying to tell me something."

Haryat was butting persistently at Mr. Bourne's chest. Nicky stroked her head.

"If it is the same donkey, she's a long way from home," he said. "I wonder where the little boy is who looks after her."

He ran a hand down her neck. Then he stopped.

"Daddy!" he said. "It *is* the same donkey."

His father came round to see what had made him so certain. Pinned to the donkey's sacking cover was a handkerchief, grimed and bulging, but still bearing in one corner the recognizable legend: *Nicholas C. Bourne*.

"Don't you remember Mummy telling you how we'd given my handkerchief to an Arab boy who'd been in a fight?"

"I do remember something of the sort." Mr. Bourne looked with a puzzled frown at the donkey. "All right, Haryat," he said. "Lead on."

Haryat tossed her head and then, as if satisfied that this was a friend, trotted a little way down the hill. After a few yards she stopped and turned to look back at them.

"She wants us to follow," said Nicky.

He moved down towards Haryat. Satisfied, she trotted on and disappeared round a rock into a side turning where the old road looped off to form a long rest area. Nicky and his father followed, and then Mr. Bourne broke into a run.

A few minutes later, Mrs. Bourne, in response to a somewhat incoherent message from a breathless Nicky, backed the Buick down the hill and pulled up beside the stop.

"Whatever's happened?" she asked.

Her husband was picking his way carefully back to the road, carrying Hamid's slight form in his arms. He laid the boy gently on the back seat of the car.

"He looks as if he's had a bad fall," she said. "There's a nasty cut on his head. I don't know how long he's been there. He's unconscious."

Mrs. Bourne was as practical as always. "Isn't there a police post at the Inn of the Good Samaritan?" she said. "They'll be able to tell us what to do. Look, I'll drive on up there with the boy. You and Nicky can follow with the donkey. It can't be very far."

"All right," agreed Mr. Bourne. "Come on, Haryat. I'll never say a donkey is stupid again."

CHAPTER TWELVE

Hamid Pays a Debt

IT WAS strange to be in a high, clean, white bed. Hamid lay for a long time, wondering at the luxury of it. The room was cool, the long, wide-open windows shaded by blinds. He turned his head and saw two rows of beds identical with his own stretching away down a long room.

He felt very peculiar—light and disembodied. He lifted a hand but let it fall back limply on the bed. Even his arms looked different. That sleeve was not his and certainly his hands had never looked so clean before. Not ever.

He struggled to attach a meaning to these mysteries, but it was too much for him. He closed his eyes and dozed again. When he awoke, there was a clean lady in white by the bedside.

"So you're awake at last," she said, smiling. "Would you like a drink?"

"Yes, please," said Hamid in a small voice.

If he spoke loudly he might shatter this beautiful dream and be back in the wilderness again, with the *khamsin* stinging his bare legs and whipping round his face.

But it was not a dream. The drink that the clean lady gave him was real. He could savor its coolness on his lips and throat. He could feel her arm where she propped him up by the shoulders. You could never do that in dreams. Nothing ever went right in dreams. Things went on and on and on, and you could not do anything about them. Like the *khamsin*. Had *that* been only a dream?

The next time he woke, he felt quite different. He sat

straight up in bed, memory rushing in on him. He still could not remember how he came to be there, but he could remember struggling up the Jerusalem road on Haryat and feeling sick and dizzy, and the heat.

If he was here, where was Haryat? And what about his appearance in court? What day was it? He struggled to climb out of bed, but the sheets were tucked in securely and before he could disentangle them, the cool, white lady was at the bedside, hushing him.

"What day is it?" he demanded. "I have to go to court. I shall be late. Where's my father?"

"Quiet, now," said the nurse. "Your father and mother are coming again later—you weren't awake when they came before. But here is someone to see you now. He will explain."

Hamid looked up, wondering, and there was Nicky, walking self-consciously between the long rows of beds, followed by his mother and father carrying a huge parcel between them.

"Hello!" Nicky said shyly. "I'm glad you're all right."

"We've just come from the court," explained Mr. Bourne. "When we got back to the hotel on Sunday, there was a note from the magistrate telling us to attend today. Nicky explained everything to him and the magistrate said I was to tell you it is quite all right. There's nothing to worry about. You have to go along next week for the charge against you to be dismissed, but it's a pure formality."

The only part of this that Hamid understood was, "It's quite all right." He let out a long sigh of relief.

"That man had to admit he took my camera," added Nicky. "But he said he did it to give me a lesson and that he was going to give it back, but I don't know whether the magistrate believed him. Anyway, I've got it back—the camera, I mean—thanks to you."

He turned questioningly to his mother and father. They

nodded.

"We've brought you this," said Nicky, helping to heave the parcel on the bed.

"For me?"

"Yes—or rather, for you and Haryat. Go on. Open it. We couldn't wait till you were out of hospital because Mummy and I go home tomorrow and we did want to see your face when you opened the parcel," said Nicky, without pausing for breath.

Hamid undid the sticky tape and string that held the parcel together and pulled back the wrapping papers. His eyes grew big with wonder.

"*Wallah!*" was all he could say.

In the parcel was a scarlet bridle and a small saddle, just big enough for a little donkey like Haryat.

"*Wallah!*" exclaimed Hamid again. Now, he thought, she'll be the smartest donkey on the Mount of Olives. Haryat will get all the customers now.

High on the balcony of the minaret, the muezzin called the faithful to the second prayer of the day.

" '*Allahu 'akbar. 'Allahu 'akbar. 'Ashadu 'anna la Ilaha illa' Allah.*"

The morning sun struck fire from the great golden dome of the Mosque of Omar. On the other side of the Kedron valley in the Garden of Gethsemane, Father Gregory sat down on the terrace steps, hitched up his brown habit and stretched out his sandalled feet to the sun. Hamid flung himself down beside him, simmering with suppressed excitement. Tourists strolling in the Garden cast an amused glance at the oddly assorted couple, but otherwise the two were undisturbed.

"Well, little Gideon?" said Father Gregory.

"I tried to be like Paul," said Hamid.

Father Gregory looked puzzled. "Like Paul?"

"Yes. The man who went to see Caesar. Only the King

wasn't there."

Father Gregory nodded understandingly. "So that's why you ran away."

Hamid looked up at him, his face radiant. "It's all right, you know. You said it would be. I kept trying to remember that."

He dived into the bosom of his *djubah* and produced a small object wrapped in a dirty white handkerchief.

"This is for you," he said, holding it out to Father Gregory. "You said I should try to make something really worthwhile."

Father Gregory unwrapped the handkerchief and lifted out the carving of Haryat, completed now and perfect in every detail. He turned it over with reverent hands, examining the exquisite workmanship that had gone into the little figure.

"The Palm Sunday donkey," he murmured. He looked across at Hamid. "Thank you, little Gideon," he said. "It's . . . it's . . . beautiful. With skill such as yours, you should have proper training. It is a gift of God to have such skill."

"The wood helped," said Hamid eagerly. "The wood was special, you remember."

"I remember," said Father Gregory, and he let his glance rest lovingly on the gnarled and ancient olive trees.

Outside the Garden of Gethsemane, Haryat stood patiently in the sunshine, nibbling at a snapdragon that had taken root in the wall. She had never looked so handsome. The police at the Inn of the Good Samaritan had given her a thorough grooming when they heard how she had led the Bournes to the rescue of Hamid. Her white coat had never been so clean, and the new scarlet bridle set it off to perfection. A group of tourists stopped to photograph her.

"What a pretty little donkey," one said. "I wonder what it's called."

Haryat rolled an eye in their direction. Her long ears

flicked at a troublesome fly. It settled on her nose, and as she shook her head to dislodge it her pendant caught the sunlight. It was almost as if she said: "Come on! Can't you read?"

GLOSSARY

"Afwan"—"You're welcome." "Don't mention it."
agal—woolen rope that holds the *keffiyeh* in place
"Ahlan wa sahlan"—"You are indeed welcome."
"Allahu akbar, Allahu akbar. Allahu akbar; ashadu an la ilaha
    illa-llah, ashadu anna Muhammedarrasullullah hayya alas-
    sala."—"Allah is great; testify that there is no God but Allah
    and Mohammed is his Prophet. Come to prayer."
"As-salaam alaykum"—"Peace be with you."
Bab Sitti Maryam—Gate of the Lady Mary
bakshhesh—alms
baclawa—pastry filled with nuts and honey
Bedouin—Arab of the desert in Asia and Africa
djubah—long, loose robe
durkbukka—elongated clay drum with skin stretched over one
    end.
Franciscan—member of a religious order founded by St. Francis
    of Assisi
Garden of Gethsemane—supposed scene of the agony and arrest
    of Christ
Gideon—Hebrew liberator and religious leader
hatta—Arab headdress consisting of the *keffiyeh* and the *agal*
"Imshi"—"Move along there." "Beat it."
"Insh' Allah—"If God wills."
keffiyeh—large kerchief worn as headdress
khamsin—hot wind, accompanied by sandstorms, that whips
    across from the Arabian desert in the spring
knaffe—honeyed cornmeal cake
laban—yogurt
lebne—soft, white, goat's milk cheese
"Marhaba"—"Hello."
matins—morning prayers
mensaf—boiled mutton and rice

Mount of Olives—a low range of hills about a half mile east of Jerusalem. According to the Bible, Jesus went down from there for His triumphal entry into Jerusalem. (Luke 19:29-44). He wept over the city and predicted its doom. Each night of His last week He returned there (Luke 21:37) until the night of His betrayal.

muezzin—the Mohammedan crier who calls Moslems to prayer five times daily, from a minaret or some high part of the mosque

"Sabah al-khayr"—"Good morning."

"Sayed"—"Sir."

"Shookran"—"Thank you."

souq—bazaar, market

Stations of the Cross—a Catholic devotion, which is divided into thirteen "stations," each one of which marks a crucial point in the passion of Christ, concluding with his burial.

"Wa 'Alaykumu s-salaam"—"And unto you, peace."

wadi—a valley that becomes a water course in the rainy season

"Wallah!"—"Goodness!" "Gosh!"

CURRENCY

1 dinar = $2.80
1,000 fils = 1 dinar or $2.80
100 fils = 28¢
10 fils = 1 piastre = 2.8¢
* value as of time of story